DOVER · THRIFT · EDITIONS

Short Stories

EDITH WHARTON

DOVER PUBLICATIONS, INC.
New York

DOVER THRIFT EDITIONS

GENERAL EDITOR: STANLEY APPELBAUM
EDITOR OF THIS VOLUME: CANDACE WARD

Copyright

Published in Canada by General Publishing Company, Ltd., 30 Lesmill Road, Don Mills, Toronto, Ontario.

Published in the United Kingdom by Constable and Company, Ltd., 3 The Lanchesters, 162–164 Fulham Palace Road, London W6 9ER.

Bibliographical Note

This Dover edition, first published in 1994, is a new selection of short stories, reprinted unabridged from standard texts of the following: *The Descent of Man* (1904; "Expiation," "The Dilettante," "The Other Two"); *The Greater Inclination* (1899; "The Muse's Tragedy," "The Pelican," "Souls Belated"); *Xingu and Other Stories* (1916; "Xingu"). An introductory Note and explanatory footnotes have been prepared specially for this edition.

Library of Congress Cataloging-in-Publication Data

Wharton, Edith, 1862–1937.
  [Short stories. Selections]
  Short stories / Edith Wharton.
    p.   cm. — (Dover thrift editions)
  ISBN 0-486-28235-X
  1. New York (N.Y.) — Social life and customs — 19th century — Fiction. I. Title. II. Series.
PS3545.H16A6   1994
813'.52 — dc20   94-32905
                                                                     CIP

Manufactured in the United States of America
Dover Publications, Inc., 31 East 2nd Street, Mineola, N.Y. 11501

Note

EDITH NEWBOLD JONES WHARTON (1862–1937) was born into one of New York's wealthier families. As befitted a young woman of her position, Wharton married at the age of twenty-three and took her place in the highest social circles of New York and Boston. In her youth Wharton, unknown to her family, wrote both poetry and fiction; as an adult she turned again to writing for the intellectual stimulus missing from her life as a young society hostess. She published her first story, "Mrs. Manstey's View," in *Scribner's* magazine in 1891, and over the next several years *Scribner's* accepted other pieces and eventually proposed a short-story volume to be published by Charles Scribner's Sons. After a long delay the collection was published in 1899, entitled *The Greater Inclination*. In her autobiography, *A Backward Glance*, Wharton describes how this publication confirmed her vocation as a writer of fiction: "I felt like some homeless waif who, after trying for years to take out naturalization papers and being rejected by every country, has finally acquired a nationality. The Land of Letters was henceforth to be my country, and I gloried in my new citizenship."

As an artist, Wharton was in a unique position to scrutinize and comment on the affluent society to which she belonged, and the short-story form was ideally suited to her talents as a social satirist. In the stories — as in many of her novels — Wharton's characters struggle against the same oppressive social conventions that she herself knew. Confronted with the limitations and expectations placed on them by themselves and others, these characters react in familiar ways. They provoke sympathy (Mrs. Anerton in "The Muse's Tragedy" and Lydia in "Souls Belated") or disdain (the title character in "The Dilettante" and the members of the Lunch Club in "Xingu") or both (Mrs. Amyot in "The Pelican," Mrs. Fetherel in "Expiation" and Waythorn in "The Other Two"). But they are never false, never boring.

While Wharton is remembered chiefly for her novels — including the Pulitzer Prize-winning *The Age of Innocence* (1920) — the short stories constitute some of her finest work, as shown by the seven stories collected here.

Contents

Expiation

I

"I CAN NEVER," said Mrs. Fetherel, "hear the bell ring without a shudder."

Her unruffled aspect — she was the kind of woman whose emotions never communicate themselves to her clothes — and the conventional background of the New York drawing room, with its pervading implication of an imminent tea tray and of an atmosphere in which the social functions have become purely reflex, lent to her declaration a relief not lost on her cousin Mrs. Clinch, who, from the other side of the fireplace, agreed, with a glance at the clock, that it *was* the hour for bores.

"Bores!" cried Mrs. Fetherel impatiently, "If I shuddered at *them*, I should have a chronic ague!"

She leaned forward and laid a sparkling finger on her cousin's shabby black knee. "I mean the newspaper clippings," she whispered.

Mrs. Clinch returned a glance of intelligence. "They've begun already?"

"Not yet; but they're sure to now, at any minute, my publisher tells me."

Mrs. Fetherel's look of apprehension sat oddly on her small features, which had an air of neat symmetry somehow suggestive of being set in order every morning by the housemaid. Someone (there were rumors that it was her cousin) had once said that Paula Fetherel would have been very pretty if she hadn't looked so like a moral axiom in a copybook hand.

Mrs. Clinch received her confidence with a smile. "Well," she said, "I suppose you were prepared for the consequences of authorship?"

Mrs. Fetherel blushed brightly. "It isn't their coming," she owned — "it's their coming *now*."

"Now?"

"The Bishop's in town."

1

Mrs. Clinch leaned back and shaped her lips to a whistle which deflected in a laugh. "Well!" she said.

"You see!" Mrs. Fetherel triumphed.

"Well — weren't you prepared for the Bishop?"

"Not now — at least, I hadn't thought of his seeing the clippings."

"And why should he see them?"

"Bella — *won't* you understand? It's John."

"John?"

"Who has taken the most unexpected tone — one might almost say out of perversity."

"Oh, perversity — " Mrs. Clinch murmured, observing her cousin between lids wrinkled by amusement. "What tone has John taken?"

Mrs. Fetherel threw out her answer with the desperate gesture of a woman who lays bare the traces of a marital fist. "The tone of being proud of my book."

The measure of Mrs. Clinch's enjoyment overflowed in laughter.

"Oh, you may laugh," Mrs. Fetherel insisted, "but it's no joke to me. In the first place, John's liking the book is so — so — such a false note — it puts me in such a ridiculous position; and then it has set him watching for the reviews — who would ever have suspected John of knowing that books were *reviewed*? Why, he's actually found out about the clipping bureau, and whenever the postman rings I hear John rush out of the library to see if there are any yellow envelopes. Of course, when they *do* come he'll bring them into the drawing room and read them aloud to everybody who happens to be here — and the Bishop is sure to happen to be here!"

Mrs. Clinch repressed her amusement. "The picture you draw is a lurid one," she conceded, "but your modesty strikes me as abnormal, especially in an author. The chances are that some of the clippings will be rather pleasant reading. The critics are not all union men."

Mrs. Fetherel stared. "Union men?"

"Well, I mean they don't all belong to the well-known Society-for-the-Persecution-of-Rising-Authors. Some of them have even been known to defy its regulations and say a good word for a new writer."

"Oh, I dare say," said Mrs. Fetherel, with the laugh her cousin's epigram exacted. "But you don't quite see my point. I'm not at all nervous about the success of my book — my publisher tells me I have no need to be — but I *am* afraid of its being a *succès de scandale*."

"Mercy!" said Mrs. Clinch, sitting up.

The butler and footman at this moment appeared with the tea tray and when they had withdrawn, Mrs. Fetherel, bending her brightly rippled head above the kettle, continued in a murmur of avowal, "The title, even, is a kind of challenge."

"*Fast and Loose*,"[1] Mrs. Clinch mused. "Yes, it ought to take."

"I didn't choose it for that reason!" the author protested. "I should have preferred something quieter — less pronounced; but I was determined not to shirk the responsibility of what I had written. I want people to know beforehand exactly what kind of book they are buying."

"Well," said Mrs. Clinch, "that's a degree of conscientiousness that I've never met with before. So few books fulfill the promise of their titles that experienced readers never expect the fare to come up to the menu."

"*Fast and Loose* will be no disappointment on that score," her cousin significantly returned. "I've handled the subject without gloves. I've called a spade a spade."

"You simply make my mouth water! And to think I haven't been able to read it yet because every spare minute of my time has been given to correcting the proofs of 'How the Birds Keep Christmas'! There's an instance of the hardships of an author's life!"

Mrs. Fetherel's eye clouded. "Don't joke, Bella, please. I suppose to experienced authors there's always something absurd in the nervousness of a new writer, but in my case so much is at stake; I've put so much of myself into this book and I'm so afraid of being misunderstood . . . of being, as it were, in advance of my time . . . like poor Flaubert. . . . I *know* you'll think me ridiculous . . . and if only my own reputation were at stake, I should never give it a thought . . . but the idea of dragging John's name through the mire. . . ."

Mrs. Clinch, who had risen and gathered her cloak about her, stood surveying from her genial height her cousin's agitated countenance.

"Why did you use John's name, then?"

"That's another of my difficulties! I *had* to. There would have been no merit in publishing such a book under an assumed name; it would have been an act of moral cowardice. *Fast and Loose* is not an ordinary novel. A writer who dares to show up the hollowness of social conventions must have the courage of her convictions and be willing to accept the consequences of defying society. Can you imagine Ibsen or Tolstoi writing under a false name?" Mrs. Fetherel lifted a tragic eye to her cousin. "You don't know, Bella, how often I've envied you since I began to write. I used to wonder sometimes — you won't mind my saying so? — why, with all your cleverness, you hadn't taken up some more exciting subject than natural history; but I see now how wise you were. Whatever happens, you will never be denounced by the press!"

"Is that what you're afraid of?" asked Mrs. Clinch, as she grasped the bulging umbrella which rested against her chair. "My dear, if I had ever

1. The title of Wharton's own first novel, written around 1877 or 1878.

had the good luck to be denounced by the press, my brougham would be waiting at the door for me at this very moment, and I shouldn't have had to ruin this umbrella by using it in the rain. Why, you innocent, if I'd ever felt the slightest aptitude for showing up social conventions, do you suppose I should waste my time writing 'Nests Ajar' and 'How to Smell the Flowers'? There's a fairly steady demand for pseudo-science and colloquial ornithology, but it's nothing, simply nothing, to the ravenous call for attacks on social institutions — especially by those inside the institutions!"

There was often, to her cousin, a lack of taste in Mrs. Clinch's pleasantries, and on this occasion they seemed more than usually irrelevant.

"*Fast and Loose* was not written with the idea of a large sale."

Mrs. Clinch was unperturbed. "Perhaps that's just as well," she returned, with a philosophic shrug. "The surprise will be all the pleasanter, I mean. For of course it's going to sell tremendously; especially if you can get the press to denounce it."

"Bella, how *can* you? I sometimes think you say such things expressly to tease me; and yet I should think you of all women would understand my purpose in writing such a book. It has always seemed to me that the message I had to deliver was not for myself alone, but for all the other women in the world who have felt the hollowness of our social shams, the ignominy of bowing down to the idols of the market, but have lacked either the courage or the power to proclaim their independence; and I have fancied, Bella dear, that, however severely society might punish me for revealing its weaknesses, I could count on the sympathy of those who, like you" — Mrs. Fetherel's voice sank — "have passed through the deep waters."

Mrs. Clinch gave herself a kind of canine shake, as though to free her ample shoulders from any drop of the element she was supposed to have traversed.

"Oh, call them muddy rather than deep," she returned; "and you'll find, my dear, that women who've had any wading to do are rather shy of stirring up mud. It sticks — especially on white clothes."

Mrs. Fetherel lifted an undaunted brow. "I'm not afraid," she proclaimed; and at the same instant she dropped her teaspoon with a clatter and shrank back into her seat. "There's the bell," she exclaimed, "and I know it's the Bishop!"

It was in fact the Bishop of Ossining, who, impressively announced by Mrs. Fetherel's butler, now made an entry that may best be described as not inadequate to the expectations the announcement raised. The Bishop always entered a room well; but, when unannounced, or preceded by a low church butler who gave him his surname, his appearance lacked the impressiveness conferred on it by the due specification of his diocesan dignity. The Bishop was very fond of his niece, Mrs. Fetherel, and one of the traits he most valued in her was the possession of a butler who knew how to announce a bishop.

Mrs. Clinch was also his niece; but, aside from the fact that she possessed no butler at all, she had laid herself open to her uncle's criticism by writing insignificant little books which had a way of going into five or ten editions, while the fruits of his own episcopal leisure — "The Wail of Jonah" (twenty cantos in blank verse), and "Through a Glass Brightly"; or, "How to Raise Funds for a Memorial Window" — inexplicably languished on the back shelves of a publisher noted for his dexterity in pushing "devotional goods." Even this indiscretion the Bishop might, however, have condoned, had his niece thought fit to turn to him for support and advice at the painful juncture of her history when, in her own words, it became necessary for her to invite Mr. Clinch to look out for another situation. Mr. Clinch's misconduct was of the kind especially designed by Providence to test the fortitude of a Christian wife and mother, and the Bishop was absolutely distended with seasonable advice and edification; so that when Bella met his tentative exhortations with the curt remark that she preferred to do her own house cleaning unassisted, her uncle's grief at her ingratitude was not untempered with sympathy for Mr. Clinch.

It is not surprising, therefore, that the Bishop's warmest greetings were always reserved for Mrs. Fetherel; and on this occasion Mrs. Clinch thought she detected, in the salutation which fell to her share, a pronounced suggestion that her own presence was superfluous — a hint which she took with her usual imperturbable good humor.

II

Left alone with the bishop, Mrs. Fetherel sought the nearest refuge from conversation by offering him a cup of tea. The Bishop accepted with the preoccupied air of a man to whom, for the moment, tea is but a subordinate incident. Mrs. Fetherel's nervousness increased; and knowing that the surest way of distracting attention from one's own affairs is to affect an interest in those of one's companion, she hastily asked if her uncle had come to town on business.

"On business — yes — " said the Bishop in an impressive tone. "I had to see my publisher, who has been behaving rather unsatisfactorily in regard to my last book."

"Ah — your last book?" faltered Mrs. Fetherel, with a sickening sense of her inability to recall the name or nature of the work in question, and a mental vow never again to be caught in such ignorance of a colleague's productions.

" 'Through a Glass Brightly,' " the Bishop explained, with an emphasis which revealed his detection of her predicament. "You may remember that I sent you a copy last Christmas?"

"Of course I do!" Mrs. Fetherel brightened. "It was that delightful story of the poor consumptive girl who had no money, and two little brothers to support — "

"Sisters — idiot sisters — " the Bishop gloomily corrected.

"I mean sisters; and who managed to collect money enough to put up a beautiful memorial window to her — her grandfather, whom she had never seen — "

"But whose sermons had been her chief consolation and support during her long struggle with poverty and disease." The Bishop gave the satisfied sigh of the workman who reviews his completed task. "A touching subject, surely; and I believe I did it justice; at least so my friends assured me."

"Why, yes — I remember there was a splendid review of it in the *Reredos!*" cried Mrs. Fetherel, moved by the incipient instinct of reciprocity.

"Yes — by my dear friend Mrs. Gollinger, whose husband, the late Dean Gollinger, was under very particular obligations to me. Mrs. Gollinger is a woman of rare literary acumen, and her praise of my book was unqualified; but the public wants more highly seasoned fare, and the approval of a thoughtful churchwoman carries less weight than the sensational comments of an illiterate journalist." The Bishop bent a meditative eye on his spotless gaiters. "At the risk of horrifying you, my dear," he added, with a slight laugh, "I will confide to you that my best chance of a popular success would be to have my book denounced by the press."

"Denounced?" gasped Mrs. Fetherel. "On what ground?"

"On the ground of immorality." The Bishop evaded her startled gaze, "Such a thing is inconceivable to you, of course; but I am only repeating what my publisher tells me. If, for instance, a critic could be induced — I mean, if a critic were to be found, who called in question the morality of my heroine in sacrificing her own health and that of her idiot sisters in order to put up a memorial window to her grandfather, it would probably raise a general controversy in the newspapers, and I might count on a sale of ten or fifteen thousand within the next year. If he described her as morbid or decadent, it might even run to twenty thousand; but that is more than I permit myself to hope. In fact I should be satisfied with any general charge of immorality." The Bishop sighed again, "I need hardly tell you that I am actuated by no mere literary ambition. Those whose opinion I most value have assured me that the book is not without merit; but, though it does not become me to dispute their verdict, I can truly say that my vanity as an author is not at stake. I have, however, a special reason for wishing to increase the circulation of 'Through a Glass Brightly'; it was written for a purpose—a purpose I have greatly at heart—"

"I know," cried his niece sympathetically. "The chantry window—?"

"Is still empty, alas! and I had great hopes that, under Providence, my little book might be the means of filling it. All our wealthy parishioners have given lavishly to the cathedral, and it was for this reason that, in writing 'Through a Glass,' I addressed my appeal more especially to the less well-endowed, hoping by the example of my heroine to stimulate the collection of small sums throughout the entire diocese, and perhaps beyond it. I am sure," the Bishop feelingly concluded, "the book would have a widespread influence if people could only be induced to read it!"

His conclusion touched a fresh threat of association in Mrs. Fetherel's vibrating nerve centers. "I never thought of that!" she cried.

The Bishop looked at her inquiringly.

"That one's books may not be read at all! How dreadful!" she exclaimed.

He smiled faintly. "I had not forgotten that I was addressing an authoress," he said. "Indeed, I should not have dared to inflict my troubles on anyone not of the craft."

Mrs. Fetherel was quivering with the consciousness of her involuntary self-betrayal. "Oh, Uncle!" she murmured.

"In fact," the Bishop continued, with a gesture which seemed to brush away her scruples, "I came here partly to speak to you about your novel. 'Fast and Loose,' I think you call it?"

Mrs. Fetherel blushed assentingly.

"And is it out yet?" the Bishop continued.

"It came out about a week ago. But you haven't touched your tea and it must be quite cold. Let me give you another cup."

"My reason for asking," the Bishop went on, with the bland inexorableness with which, in his younger days, he had been known to continue a sermon after the senior warden had looked four times at his watch, " — my reason for asking is, that I hoped I might not be too late to induce you to change the title."

Mrs. Fetherel set down the cup she had filled. "The title?" she faltered.

The Bishop raised a reassuring hand. "Don't misunderstand me, dear child; don't for a moment imagine that I take it to be in any way indicative of the contents of the book. I know you too well for that. My first idea was that it had probably been forced on you by an unscrupulous publisher. I know too well to what ignoble compromises one may be driven in such cases!" He paused, as though to give her the opportunity of confirming this conjecture, but she preserved an apprehensive silence, and he went on, as though taking up the second point in his sermon: "Or, again, the name may have taken your fancy without your realizing all that it implies to minds more alive than yours to offensive innuendoes. It is — ahem — excessively suggestive, and I hope I am not too late to warn you of the false impression it is likely to produce on the very readers whose approbation you would most value. My friend Mrs. Gollinger, for instance — "

Mrs. Fetherel, as the publication of her novel testified, was in theory a woman of independent views; and if in practice she sometimes failed to live up to her standard, it was rather from an irresistible tendency to adapt herself to her environment than from any conscious lack of moral courage. The Bishop's exordium had excited in her that sense of opposition which such admonitions are apt to provoke; but as he went on she felt herself gradually enclosed in an atmosphere in which her theories vainly gasped for breath. The Bishop had the immense dialectical advantage of invalidating any conclusions at variance with his own by always assuming that his premises were among the necessary laws of thought. This method, combined with the habit of ignoring any classifications but his own, created an element in which the first condition of existence was the immediate adoption of his standpoint; so that his niece, as she listened, seemed to feel Mrs. Gollinger's Mechlin cap spreading its conventual shadow over her rebellious brow and the *Revue de Paris* at her elbow turning into a copy of the *Reredos*. She had meant to assure her uncle that she was quite aware of the significance of the title she had chosen, that it had been deliberately selected as indicating the subject of her novel, and that the book itself had been written in direct defiance of the class of readers for whose susceptibilities he was alarmed. The words were almost on her lips when the irresistible suggestion conveyed by the Bishop's tone and language deflected them into the apologetic murmur, "Oh, Uncle, you mustn't think — I never meant — " How much farther this current of reaction might have carried her the historian is unable to compute, for at this point the door opened and her husband entered the room.

"The first review of your book!" he cried, flourishing a yellow envelope. "My dear Bishop, how lucky you're here!"

Though the trials of married life have been classified and catalogued with exhaustive accuracy, there is one form of conjugal misery which has perhaps received inadequate attention; and that is the suffering of the versatile woman whose husband is not equally adapted to all her moods. Every woman feels for the sister who is compelled to wear a bonnet which does not "go" with her gown; but how much sympathy is given to her whose husband refuses to harmonize with the pose of the moment? Scant justice has, for instance, been done to the misunderstood wife whose husband persists in understanding her; to the submissive helpmate whose taskmaster shuns every opportunity of browbeating her, and to the generous and impulsive being whose bills are paid with philosophic calm. Mrs. Fetherel, as wives go, had been fairly exempt from trials of this nature, for her husband, if undistinguished by pronounced brutality or indifference, had at least the negative merit of being her intellectual inferior. Landscape gardeners, who are aware of the usefulness of a valley in emphasizing the height of a hill, can form an idea of the account to which an accomplished woman may turn such deficiencies; and it need scarcely be said that Mrs. Fetherel had made the most of her opportunities. It was agreeably obvious to everyone, Fetherel included, that he was not the man to appreciate such a woman; but there are no limits to man's perversity, and he did his best to invalidate this advantage by admiring her without pretending to understand her. What she most suffered from was this fatuous approval; the maddening sense that, however she conducted herself, he would always admire her. Had he belonged to the class whose conversational supplies are drawn from the domestic circle, his wife's name would never have been off his lips; and to Mrs. Fetherel's sensitive perceptions his frequent silences were indicative of the fact that she was his one topic.

It was, in part, the attempt to escape this persistent approbation that had driven Mrs. Fetherel to authorship. She had fancied that even the most infatuated husband might be counted on to resent, at least negatively, an attack on the sanctity of the hearth; and her anticipations were heightened by a sense of the unpardonableness of her act. Mrs. Fetherel's relations with her husband were in fact complicated by an irrepressible tendency to be fond of him; and there was a certain pleasure in the prospect of a situation that justified the most explicit expiation.

These hopes Fetherel's attitude had already defeated. He read the book with enthusiasm, he pressed it on his friends, he sent a copy to his mother; and his very soul now hung on the verdict of the reviewers. It was perhaps this proof of his general inaptitude that made his wife doubly alive to his special defects; so that his inopportune entrance was aggravated by the very sound of his voice and the hopeless aberration of his smile. Nothing, to the observant, is more indicative of a man's character and circumstances than his way of entering a room. The Bishop of Ossining, for instance, brought with him not only an atmosphere of episcopal authority, but an implied opinion on the verbal inspiration of the Scriptures and on the attitude of the Church toward divorce; while the appearance of Mrs. Fetherel's husband produced an immediate impression of domestic felicity. His mere aspect implied that there was a well-filled nursery upstairs; that his wife, if she did not sew on his buttons, at least superintended the performance of that task; that they both went to church regularly, and that they dined with his mother every Sunday evening punctually at seven o'clock.

All this and more was expressed in the affectionate gesture with which he now raised the yellow envelope above Mrs. Fetherel's clutch; and knowing the uselessness of begging him not to be silly, she said, with a dry despair, "You're boring the Bishop horribly."

Fetherel turned a radiant eye on that dignitary. "She bores us all horribly, doesn't she, sir?" he exulted.

"Have you read it?" said his wife, uncontrollably.

"Read it? Of course not — it's just this minute come. I say, Bishop, you're not going — ?"

"Not till I've heard this," said the Bishop, settling himself in his chair with an indulgent smile.

His niece glanced at him despairingly, "Don't let John's nonsense detain you," she entreated.

"Detain him? That's good," guffawed Fetherel. "It isn't as long as one of his sermons — won't take me five minutes to read. Here, listen to this, ladies and gentlemen: 'In this age of festering pessimism and decadent depravity, it is no surprise to the nauseated reviewer to open one more volume saturated with the fetid emanations of the sewer — ' "

Fetherel, who was not in the habit of reading aloud, paused with a gasp, and the Bishop glanced sharply at his niece, who kept her gaze fixed on the teacup she had not yet succeeded in transferring to his hand.

" 'Of the sewer,' " her husband resumed; " 'but his wonder is proportionately great when he lights on a novel as sweetly inoffensive as Paula Fetherel's *Fast and Loose*. Mrs. Fetherel is, we believe, a new hand at fiction, and her work reveals frequent traces of inexperience; but these are more than atoned for by her pure fresh view of life and her altogether unfashionable regard for the reader's moral susceptibilities. Let no one be induced by its distinctly misleading title to forego the enjoyment of this pleasant picture of domestic life, which, in spite of a total lack of force in character drawing and of consecutiveness in incident, may be described as a distinctly pretty story.' "

III

It was several weeks later that Mrs. Clinch once more brought the plebeian aroma of heated tramcars and muddy street crossings into the violet-scented atmosphere of her cousin's drawing room.

"Well," she said, tossing a damp bundle of proof into the corner of a silk-cushioned bergère, "I've read it at last and I'm not so awfully shocked!"

Mrs. Fetherel, who sat near the fire with her head propped on a languid hand, looked up without speaking.

"Mercy, Paula," said her visitor, "you're ill."

Mrs. Fetherel shook her head. "I was never better," she said, mournfully.

"Then may I help myself to tea? Thanks."

Mrs. Clinch carefully removed her mended glove before taking a buttered tea cake; then she glanced again at her cousin.

"It's not what I said just now — ?" she ventured.

"Just now?"

"About *Fast and Loose?* I came to talk it over."

Mrs. Fetherel sprang to her feet. "I never," she cried dramatically, "want to hear it mentioned again!"

"Paula!" exclaimed Mrs. Clinch, setting down her cup.

Mrs. Fetherel slowly turned on her an eye brimming with the incommunicable; then, dropping into her seat again, she added, with a tragic laugh: "There's nothing left to say."

"Nothing — ?" faltered Mrs. Clinch, longing for another tea cake, but feeling the inappropriateness of the impulse in an atmosphere so charged with the portentous. "Do you mean that everything *has* been said?" She looked tentatively at her cousin. "Haven't they been nice?"

"They've been odious — odious — " Mrs. Fetherel burst out, with an ineffectual clutch at her handkerchief. "It's been perfectly intolerable!"

Mrs. Clinch, philosophically resigning herself to the propriety of taking no more tea, crossed over to her cousin and laid a sympathizing hand on that lady's agitated shoulder.

"It *is* a bore at first," she conceded; "but you'll be surprised to see how soon one gets used to it."

"I shall — never — get — used to it — " Mrs. Fetherel brokenly declared.

"Have they been so very nasty — all of them?"

"Every one of them!" the novelist sobbed.

"I'm so sorry, dear; it *does* hurt, I know — but hadn't you rather expected it?"

"Expected it?" cried Mrs. Fetherel, sitting up.

Mrs. Clinch felt her way warily. "I only mean, dear, that I fancied from what you said before the book came out that you rather expected — that you'd rather discounted — "

"Their recommending it to everybody as a perfectly harmless story?"

"Good gracious! Is *that* what they've done?"

Mrs. Fetherel speechlessly nodded.

"Every one of them?"

"Every one."

"Phew!" said Mrs. Clinch, with an incipient whistle.

"Why, you've just said it yourself!" her cousin suddenly reproached her.

"Said what?"

"That you weren't so *awfully* shocked — "

"I? Oh, well — you see, you'd keyed me up to such a pitch that it wasn't quite as bad as I expected — "

Mrs. Fetherel lifted a smile steeled for the worst. "Why not say at once," she suggested, "that it's a distinctly pretty story?"

"They haven't said *that?*"

"They've all said it."

"My poor Paula!"

"Even the Bishop — "

"The Bishop called it a pretty story?"

"He wrote me — I've his letter somewhere. The title rather scared him — he wanted me to change it; but when he'd read the book he wrote that it was all right and that he'd sent several copies to his friends."

"The old hypocrite!" cried Mrs. Clinch. "That was nothing but professional jealousy."

"Do you think so?" cried her cousin, brightening.

"Sure of it, my dear. His own books don't sell, and he knew the quickest way to kill yours was to distribute it through the diocese with his blessing."

"Then you don't really think it's a pretty story?"

"Dear me, no! Not nearly as bad as that—"

"You're so good, Bella—but the reviewers?"

"Oh, the reviewers," Mrs. Clinch jeered. She gazed meditatively at the cold remains of her tea cake. "Let me see," she said, suddenly; "do you happen to remember if the first review came out in an important paper?"

"Yes—the *Radiator*."

"That's it! I thought so. Then the others simply followed suit: they often do if a big paper sets the pace. Saves a lot of trouble. Now if you could only have got the *Radiator* to denounce you—"

"That's what the Bishop said!" cried Mrs. Fetherel.

"He did?"

"He said his only chance of selling 'Through a Glass Brightly' was to have it denounced on the ground of immorality."

"H'm," said Mrs. Clinch, "I thought he knew a trick or two." She turned an illuminated eye on her cousin. "You ought to get *him* to denounce *Fast and Loose!*" she cried.

Mrs. Fetherel looked at her suspiciously. "I suppose every book must stand or fall on its own merits," she said in an unconvinced tone.

"Bosh! That view is as extinct as the post chaise and the packet ship—it belongs to the time when people read books. Nobody does that now; the reviewer was the first to set the example, and the public was only too thankful to follow it. At first people read the reviews; now they read only the publishers' extracts from them. Even these are rapidly being replaced by paragraphs borrowed from the vocabulary of commerce. I often have to look twice before I am sure if I am reading a department store advertisement or the announcement of a new batch of literature. The publishers will soon be having their 'fall and spring openings' and their 'special importations for Horse Show Week.' But the Bishop is right, of course—nothing helps a book like a rousing attack on its morals; and as the publishers can't exactly proclaim the impropriety of their own wares, the task has to be left to the press or the pulpit."

"The pulpit?" Mrs. Fetherel mused.

"Why, yes. Look at those two novels in England last year."

Mrs. Fetherel shook her head hopelessly. "There is so much more interest in literature in England than here."

"Well, we've got to make the supply create the demand. The Bishop could run your novel up into the hundred thousands in no time."

"But if he can't make his own sell—"

"My dear, a man can't very well preach against his own writings!" Mrs. Clinch rose and picked up her proofs.

"I'm awfully sorry for you, Paula dear," she concluded, "but I can't help being thankful that there's no demand for pessimism in the field of natural history. Fancy having to write 'The Fall of a Sparrow,' or 'How the Plants Misbehave'!"

IV

Mrs. Fetherel, driving up to the Grand Central Station one morning about five months later, caught sight of the distinguished novelist, Archer Hynes, hurrying into the waiting room ahead of her. Hynes, on his side, recognizing her brougham, turned back to greet her as the footman opened the carriage door.

"My dear colleague! Is it possible that we are traveling together?"

Mrs. Fetherel blushed with pleasure. Hynes had given her two columns of praise in the *Sunday Meteor*, and she had not yet learned to disguise her gratitude.

"I am going to Ossining," she said smilingly.

"So am I. Why, this is almost as good as an elopement."

"And it will end where elopements ought to — in church."

"In church? You're not going to Ossining to go to church?"

"Why not? There's a special ceremony in the cathedral — the chantry window is to be unveiled."

"The chantry window? How picturesque! What *is* a chantry? And why do you want to see it unveiled? Are you after copy — doing something in the Huysmans manner? 'La Cathédrale,' eh?"

"Oh, no," Mrs. Fetherel hesitated. "I'm going simply to please my uncle," she said, at last.

"Your uncle?"

"The Bishop, you know." She smiled.

"The Bishop — the Bishop of Ossining? Why, wasn't he the chap who made that ridiculous attack on your book? Is that prehistoric ass your uncle? Upon my soul, I think you're mighty forgiving to travel all the way to Ossining for one of his stained-glass sociables!"

Mrs. Fetherel's smile flowed into a gentle laugh. "Oh, I've never allowed that to interfere with our friendship. My uncle felt dreadfully about having to speak publicly against my book — it was a great deal harder for him than for me — but he thought it his duty to do so. He has the very highest sense of duty."

"Well," said Hynes, with a shrug. "I don't know that he didn't do you a good turn. Look at that!"

They were standing near the bookstall and he pointed to a placard surmounting the counter and emblazoned with the conspicuous announcement: "*Fast and Loose.* New Edition with Author's Portrait. Hundred and Fiftieth Thousand."

Mrs. Fetherel frowned impatiently. "How absurd! They've no right to use my picture as a poster!"

"There's our train," said Hynes; and they began to push their way through the crowd surging toward one of the inner doors.

As they stood wedged between circumferent shoulders, Mrs. Fetherel became conscious of the fixed stare of a pretty girl who whispered eagerly to her companion. "Look, Myrtle! That's Paula Fetherel right behind us — I knew her in a minute!"

"Gracious — where?" cried the other girl, giving her head a twist which swept her Gainsborough plumes across Mrs. Fetherel's face.

The first speaker's words had carried beyond her companion's ear, and a lemon-colored woman in spectacles, who clutched a copy of the "Journal of Psychology" in one drab cotton-gloved hand, stretched her disengaged hand across the intervening barrier of humanity.

"Have I the privilege of addressing the distinguished author of *Fast and Loose?* If so, let me thank you in the name of the Woman's Psychological League of Peoria for your magnificent courage in raising the standard of revolt against —"

"You can tell us the rest in the car," said a fat man, pressing his good-humored bulk against the speaker's arm.

Mrs. Fetherel, blushing, embarrassed and happy, slipped into the space produced by this displacement, and a few moments later had taken her seat in the train.

She was a little late, and the other chairs were already filled by a company of elderly ladies and clergymen who seemed to belong to the same party, and were still busy exchanging greetings and settling themselves in their places.

One of the ladies, at Mrs. Fetherel's approach, uttered an exclamation of pleasure and advanced with outstretched hand. "My dear Mrs. Fetherel! I am so delighted to see you here. May I hope you are going to the unveiling of the chantry window? The dear Bishop so hoped that you would do so! But perhaps I ought to introduce myself. I am Mrs. Gollinger" — she lowered her voice expressively — "one of your uncle's oldest friends, one who has stood close to him through all this sad business, and who knows what he suffered when he felt obliged to sacrifice family affection to the call of duty."

Mrs. Fetherel, who had smiled and colored slightly at the beginning of this speech, received its close with a deprecating gesture.

"Oh, pray don't mention it," she murmured. "I quite understood how my uncle was placed — I bore him no ill will for feeling obliged to preach against my book."

"He understood that, and was so touched by it! He has often told me that it was the hardest task he was ever called upon to perform — and, do you know, he quite feels that this unexpected gift of the chantry window is in some way a return for his courage in preaching that sermon."

Mrs. Fetherel smiled faintly. "Does he feel that?"

"Yes; he really does. When the funds for the window were so mysteriously placed at his disposal, just as he had begun to despair of raising them, he assured me that he could not help connecting the fact with his denunciation of your book."

"Dear Uncle!" sighed Mrs. Fetherel. "Did he say that?"

"And now," continued Mrs. Gollinger, with cumulative rapture — "now that you are about to show, by appearing at the ceremony today, that there has been no break in your friendly relations, the dear Bishop's happiness will be complete. He was so longing to have you come to the unveiling!"

"He might have counted on me," said Mrs. Fetherel, still smiling.

"Ah, that is so beautifully forgiving of you!" cried Mrs. Gollinger enthusiastically. "But then, the Bishop has always assured me that your real nature was very different from that which — if you will pardon my saying so — seems to be revealed by your brilliant but — er — rather subversive book. 'If you only knew my niece, dear Mrs. Gollinger,' he always said, 'you would see that her novel was written in all innocence of heart'; and to tell you the truth, when I first read the book I didn't think it so very, *very* shocking. It wasn't till the dear Bishop had explained to me — but, dear me, I mustn't take up your time in this way when so many others are anxious to have a word with you."

Mrs. Fetherel glanced at her in surprise, and Mrs. Gollinger continued with a playful smile: "You forget that your face is familiar to thousands whom you have never seen. We all recognized you the moment you entered the train, and my friends here are so eager to make your acquaintance — even those" — her smile deepened — "who thought the dear Bishop not *quite unjustified* in his attack on your remarkable novel."

V

A religious light filled the chantry of Ossining Cathedral, filtering through the linen curtain which veiled the central window and mingling with the blaze of tapers on the richly adorned altar.

In this devout atmosphere, agreeably laden with the incense-like aroma of Easter lilies and forced lilacs, Mrs. Fetherel knelt with a sense of luxurious satisfaction. Beside her sat Archer Hynes, who had remembered that there was to be a church scene in his next novel and that his impressions of the devotional environment needed refreshing. Mrs. Fetherel was very happy. She was conscious that her entrance had sent a thrill through the female devotees who packed the chantry, and she had humor enough to enjoy the thought that, but for the good Bishop's denunciation of her book, the heads of his flock would not have been turned so eagerly in her direction. Moreover, as she entered she had caught sight of a society reporter, and she knew that her presence, and the fact that she was accompanied by Hynes, would be conspicuously proclaimed in the morning papers. All these evidences of the success of her handiwork might have turned a calmer head than Mrs. Fetherel's and though she had now learned to dissemble her gratification, it still filled her inwardly with a delightful glow.

The Bishop was somewhat late in appearing, and she employed the interval in meditating on the plot of her next novel, which was already partly sketched out, but for which she had been unable to find a satisfactory dénouement. By a not uncommon process of ratiocination, Mrs. Fetherel's success had convinced her of her vocation. She was sure now that it was her duty to lay bare the secret plague spots of society, and she was resolved that there should be no doubt as to the purpose of her new book. Experience had shown her that where she had fancied she was calling a spade a spade she had in fact been alluding in guarded terms to the drawing-room shovel. She was determined not to repeat the same mistake, and she flattered herself that her coming novel would not need an episcopal denunciation to insure its sale, however likely it was to receive this crowning evidence of success.

She had reached this point in her meditations when the choir burst into song and the ceremony of the unveiling began. The Bishop, almost always felicitous in his addresses to the fair sex, was never more so than when he was celebrating the triumph of one of his cherished purposes. There was a peculiar mixture of Christian humility and episcopal exultation in the manner with which he called attention to the Creator's promptness in responding to his demand for funds, and he had never been more happily inspired than in eulogizing the mysterious gift of the chantry window.

Though no hint of the donor's identity had been allowed to escape him, it was generally understood that the Bishop knew who had given the window, and the congregation awaited in a flutter of suspense the possible announcement of a name. None came, however, though the Bishop deliciously titillated the curiosity of his flock by circling ever closer about the interesting secret. He would not disguise from them, he said, that the heart which had divined his inmost wish had been a woman's — is it not to woman's intuitions that more than half the happiness of earth is owing? What man is obliged to learn by the laborious process of experience, woman's wondrous instinct tells her at a glance; and so it had been with this cherished scheme, this unhoped-for completion of their beautiful chantry. So much, at least, he was allowed to reveal; and indeed, had he not done so, the window itself would have spoken for him, since the first glance at its touching subject and exquisite design would show it to have originated in a woman's heart. This tribute to the sex was received with an audible sigh of contentment, and the Bishop, always stimulated by such evidence of his sway over his hearers, took up his theme with gathering eloquence.

Yes — a woman's heart had planned the gift, a woman's hand had executed it, and, might he add, without too far withdrawing the veil in which Christian beneficence ever loved to drape its acts — might he add that, under Providence, a book, a simple book, a mere tale, in fact, had had its share in the good work for which they were assembled to give thanks?

At this unexpected announcement, a ripple of excitement ran through the assemblage, and more than one head was abruptly turned in the direction of Mrs. Fetherel, who sat listening in an agony of wonder and confusion. It did not escape the observant novelist at her side that she drew down her veil to conceal an uncontrollable blush, and this evidence of dismay caused him to fix an attentive gaze on her, while from her seat across the aisle Mrs. Gollinger sent a smile of unctuous approval.

"A book — a simple book — " the Bishop's voice went on above this flutter of mingled emotions. "What is a book? Only a few pages and a little ink — and yet one of the mightiest instruments which Providence has devised for shaping the destinies of man ... one of the most powerful influences for good or evil which the Creator has placed in the hands of his creatures. . . ."

The air seemed intolerably close to Mrs. Fetherel, and she drew out her scent bottle, and then thrust it hurriedly away, conscious that she was still the center of unenviable attention. And all the while the Bishop's voice droned on. . . .

"And of all forms of literature, fiction is doubtless that which has exercised the greatest sway, for good or ill, over the passions and imagination of the masses. Yes, my friends, I am the first to acknowledge it — no sermon, however eloquent, no theological treatise, however learned and convincing, has ever inflamed the heart and imagination like a novel — a simple novel. Incalculable is the power exercised over humanity by the great magicians of the pen — a power ever enlarging its boundaries and increasing its responsibilities as popular education multiplies the number of readers. . . . Yes, it is the novelist's hand which can pour balm on countless human sufferings, or inoculate mankind with the festering poison of a corrupt imagination. . . ."

Mrs. Fetherel had turned white, and her eyes were fixed with a blind stare of anger on the large-sleeved figure in the center of the chancel.

"And too often, alas, it is the poison and not the balm which the unscrupulous hand of genius proffers to its unsuspecting readers. But, my friends, why should I continue? None know better than an assemblage of Christian women, such as I am now addressing, the beneficent or baleful influences of modern fiction; and so, when I say that this beautiful chantry window of ours owes its existence in part to the romancer's pen" — the Bishop paused, and bending forward, seemed to seek a certain face among the countenances eagerly addressed to his — "when I say that this pen, which for personal reasons it does not become me to celebrate unduly — "

Mrs. Fetherel at this point half-rose, pushing back her chair, which scraped loudly over the marble floor; but Hynes involuntarily laid a warning hand on her arm, and she sank down with a confused murmur about the heat.

"When I confess that this pen, which for once at least has proved itself so much mightier than the sword, is that which was inspired to trace the simple narrative of 'Through a Glass Brightly' " — Mrs. Fetherel looked up with a gasp of mingled relief and anger — "when I tell you, my dear friends, that it was your Bishop's own work which first roused the mind of one of his flock to the crying need of a chantry window, I think you will admit that I am justified in celebrating the triumphs of the pen, even though it be the modest instrument which your own Bishop wields."

The Bishop paused impressively, and a faint gasp of surprise and disappointment was audible throughout the chantry. Something very different from this conclusion had been expected, and even Mrs.

Gollinger's lips curled with a slightly ironic smile. But Archer Hynes's attention was chiefly reserved for Mrs. Fetherel, whose face had changed with astonishing rapidity from surprise to annoyance, from annoyance to relief, and then back again to something very like indignation.

The address concluded, the actual ceremony of the unveiling was about to take place, and the attention of the congregation soon reverted to the chancel, where the choir had grouped themselves beneath the veiled window, prepared to burst into a chant of praise as the Bishop drew back the hanging. The moment was an impressive one, and every eye was fixed on the curtain. Even Hynes's gaze strayed to it for a moment, but soon returned to his neighbor's face; and then he perceived that Mrs. Fetherel, alone of all the persons present, was not looking at the window. Her eyes were fixed in an indignant stare on the Bishop; a flush of anger burned becomingly under her veil, and her hands nervously crumpled the beautifully printed program of the ceremony.

Hynes broke into a smile of comprehension. He glanced at the Bishop, and back at the Bishop's niece; then, as the episcopal hand was solemnly raised to draw back the curtain, he bent and whispered in Mrs. Fetherel's ear:

"Why, you gave it yourself! You wonderful woman, of course you gave it yourself!"

Mrs. Fetherel raised her eyes to his with a start. Her blush deepened and her lips shaped a hasty "No"; but the denial was deflected into the indignant murmur — "It wasn't *his* silly book that did it, anyhow!"

The Dilettante

IT WAS ON an impulse hardly needing the arguments he found himself advancing in its favor, that Thursdale, on his way to the club, turned as usual into Mrs. Vervain's street.

The "as usual" was his own qualification of the act; a convenient way of bridging the interval — in days and other sequences — that lay between this visit and the last. It was characteristic of him that he instinctively excluded his call two days earlier, with Ruth Gaynor, from the list of his visits to Mrs. Vervain: the special conditions attending it had made it no more like a visit to Mrs. Vervain than an engraved dinner invitation is like a personal letter. Yet it was to talk over his call with Miss Gaynor that he was now returning to the scene of that episode; and it was because Mrs. Vervain could be trusted to handle the talking over as skillfully as the interview itself that, at her corner, he had felt the dilettante's irresistible craving to take a last look at a work of art that was passing out of his possession.

On the whole, he knew no one better fitted to deal with the unexpected than Mrs. Vervain. She excelled in the rare art of taking things for granted, and Thursdale felt a pardonable pride in the thought that she owed her excellence to his training. Early in his career, Thursdale had made the mistake, at the outset of his acquaintance with a lady, of telling her that he loved her, and exacting the same avowal in return. The latter part of that episode had been like the long walk back from a picnic, when one has to carry all the crockery one has finished using: it was the last time Thursdale ever allowed himself to be encumbered with the debris of a feast. He thus incidentally learned that the privilege of loving her is one of the least favors that a charming woman can accord; and in seeking to avoid the pitfalls of sentiment he had developed a science of evasion in which the woman of the moment became a mere implement of the game. He owed a great deal of delicate enjoyment to the cultivation of this art. The perils from which it had been his refuge became naïvely harmless: was it possible that he who now took his easy way along the levels had once preferred to gasp on the raw heights of emotion? Youth is a high-colored season; but he had the satisfaction of feeling that he had entered earlier than most into that chiaroscuro of sensation where every half-tone has its value.

As a promoter of this pleasure no one he had known was comparable to Mrs. Vervain. He had taught a good many women not to betray their feelings, but he had never before had such fine material to work with. She had been surprisingly crude when he first knew her; capable of making the most awkward inferences, of plunging through thin ice, of recklessly undressing her emotions; but she had acquired, under the discipline of his reticences and evasions, a skill almost equal to his own, and perhaps more remarkable in that it involved keeping time with any tune he played and reading at sight some uncommonly difficult passages.

It had taken Thursdale seven years to form this fine talent; but the result justified the effort. At the crucial moment she had been perfect: her way of greeting Miss Gaynor had made him regret that he had announced his engagement by letter. It was an evasion that confessed a difficulty; a deviation implying an obstacle, where, by common consent, it was agreed to see none; it betrayed, in short, a lack of confidence in the completeness of his method. It had been his pride never to put himself in a position which had to be quitted, as it were, by the back door; but here, as he perceived, the main portals would have opened for him of their own accord. All this, and much more, he read in the finished naturalness with which Mrs. Vervain had met Miss Gaynor. He had never seen a better piece of work: there was no overeagerness, no suspicious warmth, above all (and this gave her art the grace of a natural quality) there were none of those damnable implications whereby a woman, in welcoming her friend's betrothed, may keep him on pins and needles while she laps the lady in complacency. So masterly a performance, indeed, hardly needed the offset of Miss Gaynor's doorstep words — "To be so kind to me, how she must have liked you!" — though he caught himself wishing it lay within the bounds of fitness to transmit them, as a final tribute, to the one woman he knew who was unfailingly certain to enjoy a good thing. It was perhaps the one drawback to his new situation that it might develop good things which it would be impossible to hand on to Margaret Vervain.

The fact that he had made the mistake of underrating his friend's powers, the consciousness that his writing must have betrayed his distrust of her efficiency, seemed an added reason for turning down her

eet instead of going on to the club. He would show her that he knew
ow to value her; he would ask her to achieve with him a feat infinitely
rer and more delicate than the one he had appeared to avoid. Inciden-
lly, he would also dispose of the interval of time before dinner: ever
ace he had seen Miss Gaynor off, an hour earlier, on her return
urney to Buffalo, he had been wondering how he should put in the
st of the afternoon. It was absurd, how he missed the girl. . . . Yes, that
as it: the desire to talk about her was, after all, at the bottom of his
apulse to call on Mrs. Vervain! It was absurd, if you like — but it was
lightfully rejuvenating. He could recall the time when he had been
raid of being obvious: now he felt that his return to the primitive
notions might be as restorative as a holiday in the Canadian woods.
ad it was precisely by the girl's candor, her directness, her lack of
mplications, that he was taken. The sense that she might say some-
ing rash at any moment was positively exhilarating: if she had thrown
r arms about him at the station he would not have given a thought to
s crumpled dignity. It surprised Thursdale to find what freshness of
art he brought to the adventure; and though his sense of irony
evented his ascribing his intactness to any conscious purpose, he
uld but rejoice in the fact that his sentimental economies had left him
ch a large surplus to draw upon.

Mrs. Vervain was at home — as usual. When one visits the cemetery
e expects to find the angel on the tombstone, and it struck Thursdale
another proof of his friend's good taste that she had been in no undue
aste to change her habits. The whole house appeared to count on his
ming; the footman took his hat and overcoat as naturally as though
ere had been no lapse in his visits; and the drawing room at once
veloped him in that atmosphere of tacit intelligence which Mrs.
rvain imparted to her very furniture.

It was a surprise that, in this general harmony of circumstances, Mrs.
rvain should herself sound the first false note.

"You?" she exclaimed; and the book she held slipped from her
nd.

It was crude, certainly; unless it were a touch of the finest art. The
fficulty of classifying it disturbed Thursdale's balance.

"Why not?" he said, restoring the book. "Isn't it my hour?" And as she
ade no answer, he added gently, "Unless it's someone else's?"

She laid the book aside and sank back into her chair. "Mine, merely,"
e said.

"I hope that doesn't mean that you're unwilling to share it?"

"With you? By no means. You're welcome to my last crust."

He looked at her reproachfully. "Do you call this the last?"

She smiled as he dropped into the seat across the hearth. "It's a way giving it more flavor!"

He returned the smile. "A visit to you doesn't need such condiment

She took this with just the right measure of retrospective amuseme

"Ah, but I want to put into this one a very special taste," she confess

Her smile was so confident, so reassuring, that it lulled him into imprudence of saying: "Why should you want it to be different fr what was always so perfectly right?"

She hesitated. "Doesn't the fact that it's the last constitute a diff ence?"

"The last — my last visit to you?"

"Oh, metaphorically, I mean — there's a break in the continuity."

Decidedly, she was pressing too hard: unlearning his arts alrea

"I don't recognize it," he said. "Unless you make me — " he add with a note that slightly stirred her attitude of languid attention.

She turned to him with grave eyes. "You recognize no differen whatever?"

"None — except an added link in the chain."

"An added link?"

"In having one more thing to like you for — your letting Miss Gayn see why I had already so many." He flattered himself that this turn h taken the least hint of fatuity from the phrase.

Mrs. Vervain sank into her former easy pose. "Was it that you ca for?" she asked, almost gaily.

"If it is necessary to have a reason — that was one."

"To talk to me about Miss Gaynor?"

"To tell you how she talks about you."

"That will be very interesting — especially if you have seen her sin her second visit to me."

"Her second visit?" Thursdale pushed his chair back with a start a moved to another. "She came to see you again?"

"This morning, yes — by appointment."

He continued to look at her blankly. "You sent for her?"

"I didn't have to — she wrote and asked me last night. But no dou you have seen her since."

Thursdale sat silent. He was trying to separate his words from thoughts, but they still clung together inextricably. "I saw her off j now at the station."

"And she didn't tell you that she had been here again?"

"There was hardly time, I suppose — there were people about — " floundered.

"Ah, she'll write, then."

He regained his composure. "Of course she'll write: very often, I hope. You know I'm absurdly in love," he cried audaciously.

She tilted her head back, looking up at him as he leaned against the chimney piece. He had leaned there so often that the attitude touched a pulse which set up a throbbing in her throat. "Oh, my poor Thursdale!" she murmured.

"I suppose it's rather ridiculous," he owned; and as she remained silent, he added, with a sudden break — "Or have you another reason for pitying me?"

Her answer was another question. "Have you been back to your rooms since you left her?"

"Since I left her at the station? I came straight here."

"Ah, yes — you *could*: there was no reason — " Her words passed into a silent musing.

Thursdale moved nervously nearer. "You said you had something to tell me?"

"Perhaps I had better let her do so. There may be a letter at your rooms."

"A letter? What do you mean? A letter from *her*? What has happened?"

His paleness shook her, and she raised a hand of reassurance. "Nothing has happened — perhaps that is just the worst of it. You always *hated*, you know," she added incoherently, "to have things happen: you never would let them."

"And now — "

"Well, that was what she came here for: I supposed you had guessed. To know if anything had happened."

"Had happened?" He gazed at her slowly. "Between you and me?" he said with a rush of light.

The words were so much cruder than any that had ever passed between them, that the color rose to her face; but she held his startled gaze.

"You know girls are not quite as unsophisticated as they used to be. Are you surprised that such an idea should occur to her?"

His own color answered hers: it was the only reply that came to him.

Mrs. Vervain went on smoothly: "I supposed it might have struck you that there were times when we presented that appearance."

He made an impatient gesture. "A man's past is his own!"

"Perhaps — it certainly never belongs to the woman who has shared it. But one learns such truths only by experience; and Miss Gaynor is naturally inexperienced."

"Of course — but — supposing her act a natural one — " he floundered lamentably among his innuendoes "—I still don't see—how there was anything—"

"Anything to take hold of? There wasn't—"

"Well, then—?" escaped him, in undisguised satisfaction; but as she did not complete the sentence he went on with a faltering laugh: "She can hardly object to the existence of a mere friendship between us!"

"But she does," said Mrs. Vervain.

Thursdale stood perplexed. He had seen, on the previous day, no trace of jealousy or resentment in his betrothed: he could still hear the candid ring of the girl's praise of Mrs. Vervain. If she were such an abyss of insincerity as to dissemble distrust under such frankness, she must at least be more subtle than to bring her doubts to her rival for solution. The situation seemed one through which one could no longer move in a penumbra, and he let in a burst of light with the direct query: "Won't you explain what you mean?"

Mrs. Vervain sat silent, not provokingly, as though to prolong his distress, but as if, in the attenuated phraseology he had taught her, it was difficult to find words robust enough to meet his challenge. It was the first time he had ever asked her to explain anything; and she had lived so long in dread of offering elucidations which were not wanted, that she seemed unable to produce one on the spot.

At last she said slowly: "She came to find out if you were really free."

Thursdale colored again. "Free?" he stammered, with a sense of physical disgust at contact with such crassness.

"Yes—if I had quite done with you." She smiled in recovered security. "It seems she likes clear outlines; she has a passion for definitions."

"Yes—well?" he said, wincing at the echo of his own subtlety.

"Well—and when I told her that you had never belonged to me, she wanted me to define *my* status—to know exactly where I had stood all along."

Thursdale sat gazing at her intently; his hand was not yet on the clue. "And even when you had told her that—"

"Even when I had told her that I had had no status—that I had never stood anywhere, in any sense she meant," said Mrs. Vervain, slowly, "even then she wasn't satisfied, it seems."

He uttered an uneasy exclamation. "She didn't believe you, you mean?"

"I mean that she *did* believe me: too thoroughly."

"Well, then—in God's name, what did she want?"

"Something more—those were the words she used."

"Something more? Between—between you and me? Is it a conundrum?" He laughed awkwardly.

"Girls are not what they were in my day; they are no longer forbidden to contemplate the relation of the sexes."

"So it seems!" he commented. "But since, in this case, there wasn't any—" he broke off, catching the dawn of a revelation in her gaze.

"That's just it. The unpardonable offence has been—in our not offending."

He flung himself down despairingly. "I give up! What did you tell her?" he burst out with sudden crudeness.

"The exact truth. If I had only known," she broke off with a beseeching tenderness, "won't you believe that I would still have lied for you?"

"Lied for me? Why on earth should you have lied for either of us?"

"To save you—to hide you from her to the last! As I've hidden you from myself all these years!" She stood up with a sudden tragic import in her movement. "You believe me capable of that, don't you? If I had only guessed—but I have never known a girl like her; she had the truth out of me with a spring."

"The truth that you and I had never—"

"Had never—never in all these years! Oh, she knew why—she measured us both in a flash. She didn't suspect me of having haggled with you—her words pelted me like hail. 'He just took what he wanted—sifted and sorted you to suit his taste. Burnt out the gold and left a heap of cinders. And you let him—you let yourself be cut in bits'—she mixed her metaphors a little—'be cut in bits, and used or discarded, while all the while every drop of blood in you belonged to him! But he's Shylock—he's Shylock—and you have bled to death of the pound of flesh he has cut off you.' But she despises me the most, you know—far, far the most—" Mrs. Vervain ended.

The words fell strangely on the scented stillness of the room: they seemed out of harmony with its setting of afternoon intimacy, the kind of intimacy on which, at any moment, a visitor might intrude without perceptibly lowering the atmosphere. It was as though a grand opera singer had strained the acoustics of a private music room.

Thursdale stood up, facing his hostess. Half the room was between them, but they seemed to stare close at each other now that the veils of reticence and ambiguity had fallen.

His first words were characteristic: "She *does* despise me, then?" he exclaimed.

"She thinks the pound of flesh you took was a little too near the heart."

He was excessively pale. "Please tell me exactly what she said of me."

"She did not speak much of you: she is proud. But I gather that while she understands love or indifference, her eyes have never been opened to the many intermediate shades of feeling. At any rate, she expressed an unwillingness to be taken with reservations — she thinks you would have loved her better if you had loved someone else first. The point of view is original — she insists on a man with a past!"

"Oh, a past — if she's serious — I could rake up a past!" he said with a laugh.

"So I suggested: but she has her eyes on this particular portion of it. She insists on making it a test case. She wanted to know what you had done to me; and before I could guess her drift I blundered into telling her."

Thursdale drew a difficult breath. "I never supposed — your revenge is complete," he said slowly.

He heard a little gasp in her throat. "My revenge? When I sent for you to warn you — to save you from being surprised as *I* was surprised?"

"You're very good — but it's rather late to talk of saving me." He held out his hand in the mechanical gesture of leave-taking.

"How you must care! — for I never saw you so dull," was her answer. "Don't you see that it's not too late for me to help you?" And as he continued to stare, she brought out sublimely: "Take the rest — in imagination! Let it at least be of that much use to you. Tell her I lied to her — she's too ready to believe it! And so, after all, in a sense, I shan't have been wasted."

His stare hung on her, widening to a kind of wonder. She gave the look back brightly, unblushingly, as though the expedient were too simple to need oblique approaches. It was extraordinary how a few words had swept them from an atmosphere of the most complex dissimulations to this contact of naked souls.

It was not in Thursdale to expand with the pressure of fate; but something in him cracked with it, and the rift let in new light. He went up to his friend and took her hand.

"You would do it — you would do it!"

She looked at him, smiling, but her hand shook.

"Good-bye," he said, kissing it.

"Good-bye? You are going — ?"

"To get my letter."

"Your letter? The letter won't matter, if you will only do what I ask."

He returned her gaze. "I might, I suppose, without being out of character. Only, don't you see that if your plan helped me it could only harm her?"

"Harm *her*?"

"To sacrifice you wouldn't make me different. I shall go on being what I have always been — sifting and sorting, as she calls it. Do you want my punishment to fall on *her*?"

She looked at him long and deeply. "Ah, if I had to choose between you —!"

"You would let her take her chance? But I can't, you see, I must take my punishment alone."

She drew her hand away, sighing. "Oh, there will be no punishment for either of you."

"For either of us? There will be the reading of her letter for me."

She shook her head with a slight laugh. "There will be no letter."

Thursdale faced about from the threshold with fresh life in his look. "No letter? You don't mean —"

"I mean that she's been with you since I saw her — she's seen you and heard your voice. If there *is* a letter, she has recalled it — from the first station, by telegraph."

He turned back to the door, forcing an answer to her smile. "But in the meanwhile I shall have read it," he said.

The door closed on him, and she hid her eyes from the dreadful emptiness of the room.

The Muse's Tragedy

I

DANYERS AFTERWARDS liked to fancy that he had recognized Mrs. Anerton at once; but that, of course, was absurd, since he had seen no portrait of her — she affected a strict anonymity, refusing even her photograph to the most privileged — and from Mrs. Memorall, whom he revered and cultivated as her friend, he had extracted but the one impressionist phrase: "Oh, well, she's like one of those old prints where the lines have the value of color."

He was almost certain, at all events, that he had been thinking of Mrs. Anerton as he sat over his breakfast in the empty hotel restaurant, and that, looking up on the approach of the lady who seated herself at the table near the window, he had said to himself, *That might be she.*

Ever since his Harvard days — he was still young enough to think of them as immensely remote — Danyers had dreamed of Mrs. Anerton, the Silvia of Vincent Rendle's immortal sonnet cycle, the Mrs. A. of the *Life and Letters.* Her name was enshrined in some of the noblest English verse of the nineteenth century — and of all past or future centuries, as Danyers, from the standpoint of a maturer judgment, still believed. The first reading of certain poems — of the *Antinous*, the *Pia Tolomei*, the *Sonnets to Silvia* — had been epochs in Danyers' growth, and the verse seemed to gain in mellowness, in amplitude, in meaning as one brought to its interpretation more experience of life, a finer emotional sense. Where, in his boyhood, he had felt only the perfect, the almost austere beauty of form, the subtle interplay of vowel sounds, the rush and fullness of lyric emotion, he now thrilled to the close-packed significance of each line, the allusiveness of each word — his imagination lured hither and thither on fresh trails of thought, and perpetually spurred by the sense that, beyond what he had already discovered, more marvelous regions lay waiting to be explored. Danyers had written, at college, the prize essay on Rendle's poetry (it chanced to

31

be the moment of the great man's death); he had fashioned the fugitive verse of his own Storm and Stress period on the forms which Rendle had first given to English meter, and when two years later the *Life and Letters* appeared, and the Silvia of the sonnets took substance as Mrs. A., he had included in his worship of Rendle the woman who had inspired not only such divine verse but such playful, tender, incomparable prose.

Danyers never forgot the day when Mrs. Memorall happened to mention that she knew Mrs. Anerton. He had known Mrs. Memorall for a year or more, and had somewhat contemptuously classified her as the kind of woman who runs cheap excursions to celebrities; when one afternoon she remarked, as she put a second lump of sugar in his tea:

"Is it right this time? You're almost as particular as Mary Anerton."

"Mary Anerton?"

"Yes, I never *can* remember how she likes her tea. Either it's lemon *with* sugar, or lemon without sugar, or cream without either, and whichever it is must be put into the cup before the tea is poured in; and if one hasn't remembered, one must begin all over again. I suppose it was Vincent Rendle's way of taking his tea and has become a sacred rite."

"Do you *know* Mrs. Anerton?" cried Danyers, disturbed by this careless familiarity with the habits of his divinity.

" 'And did I once see Shelley plain?' Mercy, yes! She and I were at school together—she's an American, you know. We were at a *pension* near Tours for nearly a year; then she went back to New York, and I didn't see her again till after her marriage. She and Anerton spent a winter in Rome while my husband was attached to our Legation there, and she used to be with us a great deal." Mrs. Memorall smiled reminiscently. "It was *the* winter."

"The winter they first met?"

"Precisely—but unluckily I left Rome just before the meeting took place. Wasn't it too bad? I might have been in the *Life and Letters*. You know he mentions that stupid Madame Vodki, at whose house he first saw her."

"And did you see much of her after that?"

"Not during Rendle's life. You know she has lived in Europe almost entirely, and though I used to see her off and on when I went abroad, she was always so engrossed, so preoccupied, that one felt one wasn't wanted. The fact is, she cared only about his friends—she separated herself gradually from all her own people. Now, of course, it's different; she's desperately lonely; she's taken to writing to me now and then; and last year, when she heard I was going abroad, she asked me to meet her in Venice, and I spent a week with her there."

"And Rendle?"

Mrs. Memorall smiled and shook her head. "Oh, I never was allowed a peep at *him*; none of her old friends met him, except by accident. Ill-natured people say that was the reason she kept him so long. If one happened in while he was there, he was hustled into Anerton's study, and the husband mounted guard till the inopportune visitor had departed. Anerton, you know, was really much more ridiculous about it than his wife. Mary was too clever to lose her head, or at least to show she'd lost it—but Anerton couldn't conceal his pride in the conquest. I've seen Mary shiver when he spoke of Rendle as *our poet*. Rendle always had to have a certain seat at the dinner table, away from the draft and not too near the fire, and a box of cigars that no one else was allowed to touch, and a writing table of his own in Mary's sitting room—and Anerton was always telling one of the great man's idiosyncrasies: how he never would cut the ends of his cigars, though Anerton himself had given him a gold cutter set with a star sapphire, and how untidy his writing table was, and how the housemaid had orders always to bring the wastepaper basket to her mistress before emptying it, lest some immortal verse should be thrown into the dustbin."

"The Anertons never separated, did they?"

"Separated? Bless you, no. He never would have left Rendle! And besides, he was very fond of his wife."

"And she?"

"Oh, she saw he was the kind of man who was fated to make himself ridiculous, and she never interfered with his natural tendencies."

From Mrs. Memorall, Danyers further learned that Mrs. Anerton, whose husband had died some years before her poet, now divided her life between Rome, where she had a small apartment, and England, where she occasionally went to stay with those of her friends who had been Rendle's. She had been engaged, for some time after his death, in editing some juvenilia which he had bequeathed to her care; but that task being accomplished, she had been left without definite occupation, and Mrs. Memorall, on the occasion of their last meeting, had found her listless and out of spirits.

"She misses him too much—her life is too empty. I told her so—I told her she ought to marry."

"Oh!"

"Why not, pray? She's a young woman still—what many people would call young," Mrs. Memorall interjected, with a parenthetic glance at the mirror. "Why not accept the inevitable and begin over again? All the King's horses and all the King's men won't bring Rendle to life—and besides, she didn't marry *him* when she had the chance."

Danyers winced slightly at this rude fingering of his idol. Was it possible that Mrs. Memorall did not see what an anticlimax such a marriage would have been? Fancy Rendle "making an honest woman" of Silvia; for so society would have viewed it! How such a reparation would have vulgarized their past — it would have been like "restoring" a masterpiece; and how exquisite must have been the perceptions of the woman who, in defiance of appearances, and perhaps of her own secret inclination, chose to go down to posterity as Silvia rather than as Mrs. Vincent Rendle!

Mrs. Memorall, from this day forth, acquired an interest in Danyers' eyes. She was like a volume of unindexed and discursive memoirs, through which he patiently plodded in the hope of finding embedded amid layers of dusty twaddle some precious allusion to the subject of his thought. When, some months later, he brought out his first slim volume, in which the remodeled college essay on Rendle figured among a dozen somewhat overstudied "appreciations," he offered a copy to Mrs. Memorall; who surprised him, the next time they met, with the announcement that she had sent the book to Mrs. Anerton.

Mrs. Anerton in due time wrote to thank her friend. Danyers was privileged to read the few lines in which, in terms that suggested the habit of "acknowledging" similar tributes, she spoke of the author's "feeling and insight," and was "so glad of the opportunity," etc. He went away disappointed, without clearly knowing what else he had expected.

The following spring, when he went abroad, Mrs. Memorall offered him letters to everybody, from the Archbishop of Canterbury to Louise Michel. She did not include Mrs. Anerton, however, and Danyers knew, from a previous conversation, that Silvia objected to people who "brought letters." He knew also that she traveled during the summer, and was unlikely to return to Rome before the term of his holiday should be reached, and the hope of meeting her was not included among his anticipations.

The lady whose entrance broke upon his solitary repast in the restaurant of the Hotel Villa d'Este had seated herself in such a way that her profile was detached against the window, and thus viewed, her domed forehead, small arched nose, and fastidious lip suggested a silhouette of Marie Antoinette. In the lady's dress and movements — in the very turn of her wrist as she poured out her coffee — Danyers thought he detected the same fastidiousness, the same air of tacitly excluding the obvious and unexceptional. Here was a woman who had been much bored and keenly interested. The waiter brought her a *Secolo,* and as she bent above it Danyers noticed that the hair rolled back from her forehead was turning gray; but her figure was straight and slender, and she had the invaluable gift of a girlish back.

The rush of Anglo-Saxon travel had not set toward the lakes, and with the exception of an Italian family or two, and a hump-backed youth with an *abbé,* Danyers and the lady had the marble halls of the Villa d'Este to themselves.

When he returned from his morning ramble among the hills he saw her sitting at one of the little tables at the edge of the lake. She was writing, and a heap of books and newspapers lay on the table at her side. That evening they met again in the garden. He had strolled out to smoke a last cigarette before dinner, and under the black vaulting of ilexes, near the steps leading down to the boat landing, he found her leaning on the parapet above the lake. At the sound of his approach she turned and looked at him. She had thrown a black lace scarf over her head, and in this somber setting her face seemed thin and unhappy. He remembered afterwards that her eyes, as they met his, expressed not so much sorrow as profound discontent.

To his surprise she stepped toward him with a detaining gesture.

"Mr. Lewis Danyers, I believe?"

He bowed.

"I am Mrs. Anerton. I saw your name on the visitors' list and wished to thank you for an essay on Mr. Rendle's poetry — or rather to tell you how much I appreciated it. The book was sent to me last winter by Mrs. Memorall."

She spoke in even melancholy tones, as though the habit of perfunctory utterance had robbed her voice of more spontaneous accents; but her smile was charming.

They sat down on a stone bench under the ilexes, and she told him how much pleasure his essay had given her. She thought it the best in the book — she was sure he had put more of himself into it than into any other; was she not right in conjecturing that he had been very deeply influenced by Mr. Rendle's poetry? *Pour comprendre il faut aimer,*[1] and it seemed to her that, in some ways, he had penetrated the poet's inner meaning more completely than any other critic. There were certain problems, of course, that he had left untouched; certain aspects of that many-sided mind that he had perhaps failed to seize —

"But then you are young," she concluded gently, "and one could not wish you, as yet, the experience that a fuller understanding would imply."

1. *Pour . . . aimer*] To understand, it is necessary to love.

II

She stayed a month at Villa d'Este, and Danyers was with her daily. She showed an unaffected pleasure in his society; a pleasure so obviously founded on their common veneration of Rendle, that the young man could enjoy it without fear of fatuity. At first he was merely one more grain of frankincense on the altar of her insatiable divinity; but gradually a more personal note crept into their intercourse. If she still liked him only because he appreciated Rendle, she at least perceptibly distinguished him from the herd of Rendle's appreciators.

Her attitude toward the great man's memory struck Danyers as perfect. She neither proclaimed nor disavowed her identity. She was frankly Silvia to those who knew and cared; but there was no trace of the Egeria in her pose. She spoke often of Rendle's books, but seldom of himself; there was no posthumous conjugality, no use of the possessive tense, in her abounding reminiscences. Of the master's intellectual life, of his habits of thought and work, she never wearied of talking. She knew the history of each poem; by what scene or episode each image had been evoked; how many times the words in a certain line had been transposed; how long a certain adjective had been sought, and what had at last suggested it; she could even explain that one impenetrable line, the torment of critics, the joy of detractors, the last line of *The Old Odysseus*.

Danyers felt that in talking of these things she was no mere echo of Rendle's thought. If her identity had appeared to be merged in his it was because they thought alike, not because he had thought for her. Posterity is apt to regard the women whom poets have sung as chance pegs on which they hung their garlands; but Mrs. Anerton's mind was like some fertile garden wherein, inevitably, Rendle's imagination had rooted itself and flowered. Danyers began to see how many threads of his complex mental tissue the poet had owed to the blending of her temperament with his; in a certain sense Silvia had herself created the *Sonnets to Silvia*.

To be the custodian of Rendle's inner self, the door, as it were, to the sanctuary, had at first seemed to Danyers so comprehensive a privilege that he had the sense, as his friendship with Mrs. Anerton advanced, of forcing his way into a life already crowded. What room was there, among such towering memories, for so small an actuality as his? Quite suddenly, after this, he discovered that Mrs. Memorall knew better: his fortunate friend was bored as well as lonely.

"You have had more than any other woman!" he had exclaimed to her one day: and her smile flashed a derisive light on his blunder. Fool that he was, not to have seen that she had not had enough! That she was young still — do years count? — tender, human, a woman; that the living have need of the living.

After that, when they climbed the alleys of the hanging park, resting in one of the little ruined temples, or watching, through a ripple of foliage, the remote blue flash of the lake, they did not always talk of Rendle or of literature. She encouraged Danyers to speak of himself; to confide his ambitions to her; she asked him the questions which are the wise woman's substitute for advice.

"You must write," she said, administering the most exquisite flattery that human lips could give.

Of course he meant to write — why not do something great in his turn? His best, at least; with the resolve, at the outset, that his best should be *the* best. Nothing less seemed possible with that mandate in his ears. How she had divined him; lifted and disentangled his groping ambitions; laid the awakening touch on his spirit with her creative *Let there be light!*

It was his last day with her, and he was feeling very hopeless and happy.

"You ought to write a book about *him,*" she went on gently.

Danyers started; he was beginning to dislike Rendle's way of walking in unannounced.

"You ought to do it," she insisted. "A complete interpretation — a summing up of his style, his purpose, his theory of life and art. No one else could do it as well."

He sat looking at her perplexedly. Suddenly — dared he guess?

"I couldn't do it without you," he faltered.

"I could help you — I would help you, of course."

They sat silent, both looking at the lake.

It was agreed, when they parted, that he should rejoin her six weeks later in Venice. There they were to talk about the book.

III

Lago d'Iseo, August 14th.

When I said good-bye to you yesterday I promised to come back to Venice in a week: I was to give you your answer then. I was not honest in saying that; I didn't mean to go back to Venice or to see you again. I was running away from you — and I mean to keep on running! If *you* won't, *I* must. Somebody must save you from marrying a disappointed woman of — well, you say years don't count, and why should they, after all, since you are not to marry me?

That is what I dare not go back to say. *You are not to marry me.* We have had our month together in Venice (such a good month, was it not?) and now you are to go home and write a book — any book but the one we — didn't talk of! — and I am to stay here, attitudinizing among my memories like a sort of female Tithonus. The dreariness of this enforced immortality!

But you shall know the truth. I care for you, or at least for your love, enough to owe you that.

You thought it was because Vincent Rendle had loved me that there was so little hope for you. I had had what I wanted to the full; wasn't that what you said? It is just when a man begins to think he understands a woman that he may be sure he doesn't! It is because Vincent Rendle *didn't love me* that there is no hope for you. I never had what I wanted, and never, never, never will I stoop to wanting anything else.

Do you begin to understand? It was all a sham then, you say? No, it was all real as far as it went. You are young — you haven't learned, as you will later, the thousand imperceptible signs by which one gropes one's way through the labyrinth of human nature; but didn't it strike you, sometimes, that I never told you any foolish little anecdotes about him? His trick, for instance, of twirling a paper knife round and round between his thumb and forefinger while he talked; his mania for saving the backs of notes; his greediness for wild strawberries, the little pungent Alpine ones; his childish delight in acrobats and jugglers; his way of always calling me *you — dear you*, every letter began — I never told you a word of all that, did I? Do you suppose I could have helped telling you, if he had loved me? These little things would have been mine, then, a part of my life — of our life — they would have slipped out in spite of me (it's only your unhappy woman who is always reticent and dignified). But there never was any "our life"; it was always "our lives" to the end. . . .

If you knew what a relief it is to tell someone at last, you would bear with me, you would let me hurt you! I shall never be quite so lonely again, now that someone knows.

Let me begin at the beginning. When I first met Vincent Rendle I was not twenty-five. That was twenty years ago. From that time until his death, five years ago, we were fast friends. He gave me fifteen years, perhaps the best fifteen years, of his life. The world, as you know, thinks that his greatest poems were written during those years; I am supposed to have "inspired" them, and in a sense I did. From the first, the intellectual sympathy between us was almost complete; my mind must have been to him (I fancy) like some perfectly tuned instrument on which he was never tired of playing. Someone told me of his once saying of me that I "always understood"; it is the only praise I ever heard of his giving me. I don't even know if he thought me pretty, though I hardly think my appearance could have been disagreeable to him, for he hated to be with ugly people. At all events he fell into the way of spending more and more of his time with me. He liked our house; our ways suited him. He was nervous, irritable; people bored him and yet he disliked solitude. He took sanctuary with us. When we traveled he went with us; in the winter he took rooms near us in Rome. In England or on the continent he was always with us for a good part of the year. In small ways I was able to help him in his work; he grew dependent on me. When we were apart he wrote to me continually—he liked to have me share in all he was doing or thinking; he was impatient for my criticism of every new book that interested him; I was a part of his intellectual life. The pity of it was that I wanted to be something more. I was a young woman and I was in love with him—not because he was Vincent Rendle, but just because he was himself!

People began to talk, of course—I was Vincent Rendle's Mrs. Anerton; when the *Sonnets to Silvia* appeared, it was whispered that I was Silvia. Wherever he went, I was invited; people made up to me in the hope of getting to know him; when I was in London my doorbell never stopped ringing. Elderly peeresses, aspiring hostesses, lovesick girls and struggling authors overwhelmed me with their assiduities. I hugged my success, for I knew what it meant—they thought that Rendle was in love with me! Do you know, at times, they almost made me think so too? Oh, there was no phase of folly I didn't go through. You can't imagine the excuses a woman will invent for a man's not telling her that he loves her—pitiable arguments that she would see through at a glance if any other woman used them! But all the while, deep down, I knew he had never cared. I should have known it if he had made love to me every day of his life. I could never guess whether he knew what people said about us—he listened so little to what people said; and cared still less, when he heard. He was always quite honest and straightforward with me; he treated me as one man treats another; and yet at times I felt he *must* see that with me it was different. If he did see, he made no sign. Perhaps he never noticed—I am sure he never meant to be cruel. He had never made love to me; it was no fault of his if I wanted more than he could give me. The *Sonnets to Silvia*, you say? But what are they? A cosmic philosophy, not a love poem; addressed to Woman, not to a woman!

But then, the letters? Ah, the letters! Well, I'll make a clean breast of it. You have noticed the breaks in the letters here and there, just as they seem to be on the point of growing a little — warmer? The critics, you may remember, praised the editor for his commendable delicacy and good taste (so rare in these days!) in omitting from the correspondence all personal allusions, all those *détails intimes* which should be kept sacred from the public gaze. They referred, of course, to the asterisks in the letters to Mrs. A. Those letters I myself prepared for publication; that is to say, I copied them out for the editor, and every now and then I put in a line of asterisks to make it appear that something had been left out. You understand? The asterisks were a sham — *there was nothing to leave out.*

No one but a woman could understand what I went through during those years — the moments of revolt, when I felt I must break away from it all, fling the truth in his face and never see him again; the inevitable reaction, when not to see him seemed the one unendurable thing, and I trembled lest a look or word of mine should disturb the poise of our friendship; the silly days when I hugged the delusion that he *must* love me, since everybody thought he did; the long periods of numbness, when I didn't seem to care whether he loved me or not. Between these wretched days came others when our intellectual accord was so perfect that I forgot everything else in the joy of feeling myself lifted up on the wings of his thought. Sometimes, then, the heavens seemed to be opened.

All this time he was so dear a friend! He had the genius of friendship, and he spent it all on me. Yes, you were right when you said that I have had more than any other woman. *Il faut de l'adresse pour aimer,*[2] Pascal says; and I was so quiet, so cheerful, so frankly affectionate with him, that in all those years I am almost sure I never bored him. Could I have hoped as much if he had loved me?

You mustn't think of him, though, as having been tied to my skirts. He came and went as he pleased, and so did his fancies. There was a girl once (I am telling you everything), a lovely being who called his poetry "deep" and gave him *Lucile* on his birthday. He followed her to Switzerland one summer, and all the time that he was dangling after her (a little too conspicuously, I always thought, for a Great Man), he was writing to *me* about his theory of vowel combinations — or was it his experiments in English hexameter? The letters were dated from the very places where I knew they went and sat by waterfalls together and he thought out adjectives for her hair. He talked to me about it quite frankly

2. *Il faut . . . aimer*] It takes skill to love.

afterwards. She was perfectly beautiful and it had been a pure delight to watch her; but she *would* talk, and her mind, he said, was "all elbows." And yet, the next year, when her marriage was announced, he went away alone, quite suddenly . . . and it was just afterwards that he published *Love's Viaticum.* Men are queer!

After my husband died — I am putting things crudely, you see — I had a return of hope. It was because he loved me, I argued, that he had never spoken; because he had always hoped some day to make me his wife; because he wanted to spare me the "reproach." Rubbish! I knew well enough, in my heart of hearts, that my one chance lay in the force of habit. He had grown used to me; he was no longer young; he dreaded new people and new ways; *il avait pris son pli.*[3] Would it not be easier to marry me?

I don't believe he ever thought of it. He wrote me what people call "a beautiful letter"; he was kind, considerate, decently commiserating; then, after a few weeks, he slipped into his old way of coming in every afternoon, and our interminable talks began again just where they had left off. I heard later that people thought I had shown "such good taste" in not marrying him.

So we jogged on for five years longer. Perhaps they were the best years, for I had given up hoping. Then he died.

After his death — this is curious — there came to me a kind of mirage of love. All the books and articles written about him, all the reviews of the *Life,* were full of discreet allusions to Silvia. I became again the Mrs. Anerton of the glorious days. Sentimental girls and dear lads like you turned pink when somebody whispered, "That was Silvia you were talking to." Idiots begged for my autograph — publishers urged me to write my reminiscences of him — critics consulted me about the reading of doubtful lines. And I knew that, to all these people, I was the woman Vincent Rendle had loved.

After a while that fire went out too and I was left alone with my past. Alone — quite alone; for he had never really been with me. The intellectual union counted for nothing now. It had been soul to soul, but never hand in hand, and there were no little things to remember him by.

Then there set in a kind of Arctic winter. I crawled into myself as into a snow hut. I hated my solitude and yet dreaded anyone who disturbed it. That phase, of course, passed like the others. I took up life again, and began to read the papers and consider the cut of my gowns. But here was one question that I could not be rid of, that haunted me night and day. Why had he never loved me? Why had I been so much to him, and no

3. *il avait . . . pli*] he had formed the habit.

more? Was I so ugly, so essentially unlovable, that though a man might cherish me as his mind's comrade, he could not care for me as a woman? I can't tell you how that question tortured me. It became an obsession.

My poor friend, do you begin to see? I had to find out what some other man thought of me. Don't be too hard on me! Listen first — consider. When I first met Vincent Rendle I was a young woman, who had married early and led the quietest kind of life; I had had no "experiences." From the hour of our first meeting to the day of his death I never looked at any other man, and never noticed whether any other man looked at me. When he died, five years ago, I knew the extent of my powers no more than a baby. Was it too late to find out? Should I never know *why*?

Forgive me — forgive me. You are so young; it will be an episode, a mere "document," to you so soon! And, besides, it wasn't as deliberate, as cold-blooded as these disjointed lines have made it appear. I didn't plan it, like a woman in a book. Life is so much more complex than any rendering of it can be. I liked you from the first — I was drawn to you (you must have seen that) — I wanted you to like me; it was not a mere psychological experiment. And yet in a sense it was that, too — I must be honest. I had to have an answer to that question; it was a ghost that had to be laid.

At first I was afraid — oh, so much afraid — that you cared for me only because I was Silvia, that you loved me because you thought Rendle had loved me. I began to think there was no escaping my destiny.

How happy I was when I discovered that you were growing jealous of my past; that you actually hated Rendle! My heart beat like a girl's when you told me you meant to follow me to Venice.

After our parting at Villa d'Este my old doubts reasserted themselves. What did I know of your feeling for me, after all? Were you capable of analyzing it yourself? Was it not likely to be two-thirds vanity and curiosity, and one-third literary sentimentality? You might easily fancy that you cared for Mary Anerton when you were really in love with Silvia — the heart is such a hypocrite! Or you might be more calculating than I had supposed. Perhaps it was you who had been flattering *my* vanity in the hope (the pardonable hope!) of turning me, after a decent interval, into a pretty little essay with a margin.

When you arrived in Venice and we met again — do you remember the music on the lagoon, that evening, from my balcony? — I was so afraid you would begin to talk about the book — the book, you remember, was your ostensible reason for coming. You never spoke of it, and I soon saw your one fear was *I* might do so — might remind you of your object in being with me. Then I knew you cared for me! yes, at that moment really cared! We never mentioned the book once, did we, during that month in Venice?

I have read my letter over; and now I wish that I had said this to you instead of writing it. I could have felt my way then, watching your face and seeing if you understood. But, no, I could not go back to Venice; and I could not tell you (though I tried) while we were there together. I couldn't spoil that month — my one month. It was so good, for once in my life, to get away from literature.

You will be angry with me at first — but, alas! not for long. What I have done would have been cruel if I had been a younger woman; as it is, the experiment will hurt no one but myself. And it will hurt me horribly (as much as, in your first anger, you may perhaps wish), because it has shown me, for the first time, all that I have missed.

The Pelican

SHE WAS VERY pretty when I first knew her, with the sweet straight nose and short upper lip of the cameo-brooch divinity, humanized by a dimple that flowered in her cheek whenever anything was said possessing the outward attributes of humor without its intrinsic quality. For the dear lady was providentially deficient in humor: the least hint of the real thing clouded her lovely eye like the hovering shadow of an algebraic problem.

I don't think nature had meant her to be "intellectual"; but what can a poor thing do, whose husband has died of drink when her baby is hardly six months old, and who finds her coral necklace and her grandfather's edition of the British Dramatists inadequate to the demands of the creditors?

Her mother, the celebrated Irene Astarte Pratt, had written a poem in blank verse on "The Fall of Man"; one of her aunts was dean of a girls' college; another had translated Euripides — with such a family, the poor child's fate was sealed in advance. The only way of paying her husband's debts and keeping the baby clothed was to be intellectual; and, after some hesitation as to the form her mental activity was to take, it was unanimously decided that she was to give lectures.

They began by being drawing-room lectures. The first time I saw her she was standing by the piano, against the flippant background of Dresden china and photographs, telling a roomful of women preoccupied with their spring bonnets all she thought she knew about Greek art. The ladies assembled to hear her had given me to understand that she was "doing it for the baby," and this fact, together with the shortness of her upper lip and the bewildering co-operation of her dimple, disposed me to listen leniently to her dissertation. Happily, at that time Greek art was still, if I may use the phrase, easily handled: it was as simple as walking down a museum gallery lined with pleasant familiar

45

Venuses and Apollos. All the later complications — the archaic and archaistic conundrums; the influences of Assyria and Asia Minor; the conflicting attributions and the wrangles of the erudite — still slumbered in the bosom of the future "scientific critic." Greek art in those days began with Phidias and ended with the Apollo Belvedere; and a child could travel from one to the other without danger of losing his way.

Mrs. Amyot had two fatal gifts: a capacious but inaccurate memory, and an extraordinary fluency of speech. There was nothing she did not remember — wrongly; but her halting facts were swathed in so many layers of rhetoric that their infirmities were imperceptible to her friendly critics. Besides, she had been taught Greek by the aunt who had translated Euripides; and the mere sound of the *aís* and *oís* that she now and then not unskillfully let slip (correcting herself, of course, with a start, and indulgently mistranslating the phrase), struck awe to the hearts of ladies whose only "accomplishment" was French — if you didn't speak too quickly.

I had then but a momentary glimpse of Mrs. Amyot, but a few months later I came upon her again in the New England university town where the celebrated Irene Astarte Pratt lived on the summit of a local Parnassus, with lesser muses and college professors respectfully grouped on the lower ledges of the sacred declivity. Mrs. Amyot, who, after her husband's death, had returned to the maternal roof (even during her father's lifetime the roof had been distinctively maternal); Mrs. Amyot, thanks to her upper lip, her dimple and her Greek, was already ensconced in a snug hollow of the Parnassian slope.

After the lecture was over it happened that I walked home with Mrs. Amyot. From the incensed glances of two or three learned gentlemen who were hovering on the doorstep when we emerged, I inferred that Mrs. Amyot, at that period, did not often walk home alone; but I doubt whether any of my discomfited rivals, whatever his claims to favor, was ever treated to so ravishing a mixture of shyness and self-abandonment, of sham erudition and real teeth and hair, as it was my privilege to enjoy. Even at the opening of her public career Mrs. Amyot had a tender eye for strangers, as possible links with successive centers of culture to which in due course the torch of Greek art might be handed on.

She began by telling me that she had never been so frightened in her life. She knew, of course, how dreadfully learned I was, and when, just as she was going to begin, her hostess had whispered to her that I was in the room, she had felt ready to sink through the floor. Then (with a flying dimple) she had remembered Emerson's line — wasn't it Emerson's? — that beauty is its own excuse for *seeing*, and that had made her feel a little more confident, since she was sure that no one *saw* beauty more vividly than she — as a child she used to sit for hours gazing at an Etruscan vase on the bookcase in the library, while her sisters played with their dolls — and if *seeing* beauty was the only excuse one needed for talking about it, why, she was sure I would make allowances and not be *too* critical and sarcastic, especially if, as she thought probable, I had heard of her having lost her poor husband, and how she had to do it for the baby.

Being abundantly assured of my sympathy on these points, she went on to say that she had always wanted so much to consult me about her lectures. Of course, one subject wasn't enough (this view of the limitations of Greek art as a "subject" gave me a startling idea of the rate at which a successful lecturer might exhaust the universe); she must find others; she had not ventured on any as yet, but she had thought of Tennyson — didn't I *love* Tennyson? She *worshiped* him so that she was sure she could help others to understand him: or what did I think of a "course" on Raphael or Michelangelo — or on the heroines of Shakespeare? There were some fine steel engravings of Raphael's Madonnas and of the Sistine ceiling in her mother's library, and she had seen Miss Cushman in several Shakespearian roles, so that on these subjects also she felt qualified to speak with authority.

When we reached her mother's door she begged me to come in and talk the matter over; she wanted me to see the baby — she felt as though I should understand her better if I saw the baby — and the dimple flashed through a tear.

The fear of encountering the author of "The Fall of Man," combined with the opportune recollection of a dinner engagement, made me evade this appeal with the promise of returning on the morrow. On the morrow, I left too early to redeem my promise; and for several years afterwards I saw no more of Mrs. Amyot.

My calling at that time took me at irregular intervals from one to another of our larger cities, and as Mrs. Amyot was also peripatetic it was inevitable that sooner or later we should cross each other's path. It was therefore without surprise that, one snowy afternoon in Boston, I learned from the lady with whom I chanced to be lunching that, as soon as the meal was over, I was to be taken to hear Mrs. Amyot lecture.

"On Greek art?" I suggested.

"Oh, you've heard her then? No, this is one of the series called 'Homes and Haunts of the Poets.' Last week we had Wordsworth and the Lake Poets, today we are to have Goethe and Weimar. She is a wonderful creature — all the women of her family are geniuses. You know, of course, that her mother was Irene Astarte Pratt, who wrote a poem on 'The Fall of Man'; N. P. Willis called her the female Milton of America. One of Mrs. Amyot's aunts has translated Eurip —"

"And is she as pretty as ever?" I irrelevantly interposed.

My hostess looked shocked. "She is excessively modest and retiring. She says it is actual suffering for her to speak in public. You know she only does it for the baby."

Punctually at the hour appointed, we took our seats in a lecture hall full of strenuous females in ulsters. Mrs. Amyot was evidently a favorite with these austere sisters, for every corner was crowded, and as we entered a pale usher with an educated mispronunciation was setting forth to several dejected applicants the impossibility of supplying them with seats.

Our own were happily so near the front that when the curtains at the back of the platform parted, and Mrs. Amyot appeared, I was at once able to establish a comparison between the lady placidly dimpling to the applause of her public and the shrinking drawing-room orator of my earlier recollections.

Mrs. Amyot was as pretty as ever, and there was the same curious discrepancy between the freshness of her aspect and the staleness of her theme, but something was gone of the blushing unsteadiness with which she had fired her first random shots at Greek art. It was not that the shots were less uncertain, but that she now had an air of assuming that, for her purpose, the bull's-eye was everywhere, so that there was no need to be flustered in taking aim. This assurance had so facilitated the flow of her eloquence that she seemed to be performing a trick analogous to that of the conjurer who pulls hundreds of yards of white paper out of his mouth. From a large assortment of stock adjectives she chose, with unerring deftness and rapidity, the one that taste and discrimination would most surely have rejected, fitting out her subject with a whole wardrobe of slop-shop epithets irrelevant in cut and size. To the invaluable knack of not disturbing the association of ideas in her audience, she added the gift of what may be called a confidential manner — so that her fluent generalizations about Goethe and his place in literature (the lecture was, of course, manufactured out of Lewes's book) had the flavor of personal experience, of views sympathetically exchanged with her audience on the best way of knitting children's socks, or of putting up preserves for the winter. It was, I am sure, to this personal accent — the moral equivalent of her dimple — that Mrs. Amyot owed her prodigious, her irrational success. It was her art of transposing secondhand ideas into firsthand emotions that so endeared her to her feminine listeners.

To anyone not in search of "documents" Mrs. Amyot's success was hardly of a kind to make her more interesting, and my curiosity flagged with the growing conviction that the "suffering" entailed on her by public speaking was at most a retrospective pang. I was sure that she had reached the point of measuring and enjoying her effects, of deliberately manipulating her public; and there must indeed have been a certain exhilaration in attaining results so considerable by means involving so little conscious effort. Mrs. Amyot's art was simply an extension of coquetry: she flirted with her audience.

In this mood of enlightened skepticism I responded but languidly to my hostess' suggestion that I should go with her that evening to see Mrs. Amyot. The aunt who had translated Euripides was at home on Saturday evenings, and one met "thoughtful" people there, my hostess explained: it was one of the intellectual centers of Boston. My mood remained distinctly resentful of any connection between Mrs. Amyot and intellectuality, and I declined to go; but the next day I met Mrs. Amyot in the street.

She stopped me reproachfully. She had heard I was in Boston; why had I not come last night? She had been told that I was at her lecture, and it had frightened her — yes, really, almost as much as years ago in Hillbridge. She never *could* get over that stupid shyness, and the whole business was as distasteful to her as ever; but what could she do? There was the baby — he was a big boy now, and boys were *so* expensive! But did I really think she had improved the least little bit? And why wouldn't I come home with her now, and see the boy, and tell her frankly what I had thought of the lecture? She had plenty of flattery — people were *so* kind, and everyone knew that she did it for the baby — but what she felt the need of was criticism, severe, discriminating criticism like mine — oh, she knew that I was dreadfully discriminating!

I went home with her and saw the boy. In the early heat of her Tennyson worship Mrs. Amyot had christened him Lancelot, and he looked it. Perhaps, however, it was his black velvet dress and the exasperating length of his yellow curls, together with the fact of his having been taught to recite Browning to visitors, that raised to fever heat the itching of my palms in his Infant Samuel-like presence. I have since had reason to think that he would have preferred to be called Billy, and to hunt cats with the other boys in the block: his curls and his poetry were simply another outlet for Mrs. Amyot's irrepressible coquetry.

But if Lancelot was not genuine, his mother's love for him was. It justified everything — the lectures *were* for the baby, after all. I had not been ten minutes in the room before I was pledged to help Mrs. Amyot carry out her triumphant fraud. If she wanted to lecture on Plato she should — Plato must take his chance like the rest of us! There was no use, of course, in being "discriminating." I preserved sufficient reason to avoid that pitfall, but I suggested "subjects" and made lists of books for her with a fatuity that became more obvious as time attenuated the remembrance of her smile; I even remember thinking that some men might have cut the knot by marrying her, but I handed over Plato as a hostage and escaped by the afternoon train.

The next time I saw her was in New York, when she had become so fashionable that it was a part of the whole duty of woman to be seen at her lectures. The lady who suggested that of course I ought to go and hear Mrs. Amyot, was not very clear about anything except that she was perfectly lovely, and had had a horrid husband, and was doing it to support her boy. The subject of the discourse (I think it was on Ruskin) was clearly of minor importance, not only to my friend, but to the throng of well-dressed and absent-minded ladies who rustled in late, dropped their muffs, and pocketbooks, and undisguisedly lost themselves in the study of each other's apparel. They received Mrs. Amyot with warmth, but she evidently represented a social obligation like going to church, rather than any more personal interest; in fact, I suspect that every one of the ladies would have remained away, had they been sure that none of the others were coming.

Whether Mrs. Amyot was disheartened by the lack of sympathy between herself and her hearers, or whether the sport of arousing it had become a task, she certainly imparted her platitudes with less convincing warmth than of old. Her voice had the same confidential inflections, but it was like a voice reproduced by a gramophone: the real woman seemed far away. She had grown stouter without losing her dewy freshness, and her smart gown might have been taken to show either the potentialities of a settled income, or a politic concession to the taste of her hearers. As I listened I reproached myself for ever having suspected her of self-deception in saying that she took no pleasure in her work. I was sure now that she did it only for Lancelot, and judging from the size of her audience and the price of the tickets I concluded that Lancelot must be receiving a liberal education.

I was living in New York that winter, and in the rotation of dinners I found myself one evening at Mrs. Amyot's side. The dimple came out at my greeting as punctually as a cuckoo in a Swiss clock, and I detected the same automatic quality in the tone in which she made her usual pretty demand for advice. She was like a musical box charged with popular airs. They succeeded one another with breathless rapidity, but there was a moment after each when the cylinders scraped and whizzed.

Mrs. Amyot, as I found when I called on her, was living in a sunny flat, with a sitting room of flowers and a tea table that had the air of expecting visitors. She owned that she had been ridiculously successful. It was delightful, of course, on Lancelot's account. Lancelot had been sent to the best school in the country, and if things went well and people didn't tire of his silly mother he was to go to Harvard afterwards. During the next two or three years Mrs. Amyot kept her flat in New York, and radiated art and literature upon the suburbs. I saw her now and then, always stouter, better dressed, more successful and more automatic: she had become a lecturing machine.

I went abroad for a year or two and when I came back she had disappeared. I asked several people about her, but life had closed over her. She had been last heard of as lecturing — still lecturing — but no one seemed to know when or where.

It was in Boston that I found her at last, forlornly swaying to the oscillations of an overhead strap in a crowded trolley car. Her face had so changed that I lost myself in a startled reckoning of the time that had elapsed since our parting. She spoke to me shyly, as though aware of my hurried calculation, and conscious that in five years she ought not to have altered so much as to upset my notion of time. Then she seemed to set it down to her dress, for she nervously gathered her cloak over a gown that asked only to be concealed, and shrank into a seat behind the line of prehensile bipeds blocking the aisle of the car.

It was perhaps because she so obviously avoided me that I felt for the first time that I might be of use to her; and when she left the car I made no excuse for following her.

She said nothing of needing advice and did not ask me to walk home with her, concealing, as we talked, her transparent preoccupations under the guise of a sudden interest in all I had been doing since she had last seen me. Of what concerned her, I learned only that Lancelot was well and that for the present, she was not lecturing — she was tired and her doctor had ordered her to rest. On the doorstep of a shabby house she paused and held out her hand. She had been so glad to see me and perhaps if I were in Boston again — the tired dimple, as it were, bowed me out and closed the door on the conclusion of the phrase.

Two or three weeks later, at my club in New York, I found a letter from her. In it she owned that she was troubled, that of late she had been unsuccessful, and that, if I chanced to be coming back to Boston, and could spare her a little of that invaluable advice which — . A few days later the advice was at her disposal. She told me frankly what had happened. Her public had grown tired of her. She had seen it coming on for some time, and was shrewd enough in detecting the causes. She had more rivals than formerly — younger women, she admitted, with a smile that could still afford to be generous — and then her audiences had grown more critical and consequently more exacting. Lecturing — as she understood it — used to be simple enough. You chose your topic —

Raphael, Shakespeare, Gothic Architecture, or some such big familiar "subject" — and read up about it for a week or so at the Athenaeum or the Astor Library, and then told your audience what you had read. Now, it appeared, that simple process was no longer adequate. People had tired of familiar "subjects"; it was the fashion to be interested in things that one hadn't always known about — natural selection, animal magnetism, sociology and comparative folklore; while, in literature, the demand had become equally difficult to meet, since Matthew Arnold had introduced the habit of studying the "influence" of one author on another. She had tried lecturing on influences, and had done very well as long as the public was satisfied with the tracing of such obvious influences as that of Turner on Ruskin, of Schiller on Goethe, of Shakespeare on English literature; but such investigations had soon lost all charm for her too-sophisticated audiences, who now demanded either that the influence or the influenced should be quite unknown, or that there should be no perceptible connection between the two. The zest of the performance lay in the measure of ingenuity with which the lecturer established a relation between two people who had probably never heard of each other, much less read each other's works. A pretty Miss Williams with red hair had, for instance, been lecturing with great success on the influence of the Rosicrucians upon the poetry of Keats, while somebody else had given a "course" on the influence of St. Thomas Aquinas upon Professor Huxley.

Mrs. Amyot, warmed by my participation in her distress, went on to say that the growing demand for evolution was what most troubled her. Her grandfather had been a pillar of the Presbyterian ministry, and the idea of her lecturing on Darwin or Herbert Spencer was deeply shocking to her mother and aunts. In one sense the family had staked its literary as well as its spiritual hopes on the literal inspiration of Genesis: what became of "The Fall of Man" in the light of modern exegesis?

The upshot of it was that she had ceased to lecture because she could no longer sell tickets enough to pay for the hire of a lecture hall; and as for the managers, they wouldn't look at her. She had tried her luck all through the Eastern States and as far south as Washington; but it was of no use, and unless she could get hold of some new subjects — or, better still, of some new audiences — she must simply go out of the business. That would mean the failure of all she had worked for, since Lancelot would have to leave Harvard. She paused, and wept some of the unbecoming tears that spring from real grief. Lancelot, it appeared, was to be a genius. He had passed his opening examinations brilliantly; he had "literary gifts"; he had written beautiful poetry, much of which his mother had copied out, in reverentially slanting characters, in a velvet-bound volume which she drew from a locked drawer.

Lancelot's verse struck me as nothing more alarming than growing pains; but it was not to learn this that she had summoned me. What she wanted was to be assured that he was worth working for, an assurance which I managed to convey by the simple stratagem of remarking that the poems reminded me of Swinburne — and so they did, as well as of Browning, Tennyson, Rossetti, and all the other poets who supply young authors with original inspirations.

This point being established, it remained to be decided by what means his mother was, in the French phrase, to pay herself the luxury of a poet. It was clear that this indulgence could be bought only with counterfeit coin, and that the one way of helping Mrs. Amyot was to become a party to the circulation of such currency. My fetish of intellectual integrity went down like a ninepin before the appeal of a woman no longer young and distinctly foolish, but full of those dear contradictions and irrelevancies that will always make flesh and blood prevail against a syllogism. When I took leave of Mrs. Amyot I had promised her a dozen letters to Western universities and had half pledged myself to sketch out a lecture on the reconciliation of science and religion.

In the West she achieved a success which for a year or more embittered my perusal of the morning papers. The fascination that lures the murderer back to the scene of his crime drew my eye to every paragraph celebrating Mrs. Amyot's last brilliant lecture on the influence of something upon somebody; and her own letters — she overwhelmed me with them — spared me no detail of the entertainment given in her honor by the Palimpsest Club of Omaha or of her reception at the University of Leadville. The college professors were especially kind: she assured me that she had never before met with such discriminating sympathy. I winced at the adjective, which cast a sudden light on the vast machinery of fraud that I had set in motion. All over my native land, men of hitherto unblemished integrity were conniving with me in urging their friends to go and hear Mrs. Amyot lecture on the reconciliation of science and religion! My only hope was that, somewhere among the number of my accomplices, Mrs. Amyot might find one who would marry her in the defense of his convictions.

None, apparently, resorted to such heroic measures; for about two years later I was startled by the announcement that Mrs. Amyot was lecturing in Trenton, New Jersey, on modern theosophy in the light of the Vedas. The following week she was at Newark, discussing Schopenhauer in the light of recent psychology. The week after that I was on the deck of an ocean steamer, reconsidering my share in Mrs. Amyot's triumphs with the impartiality with which one views an episode that is being left behind at the rate of twenty knots an hour. After all, I had been helping a mother to educate her son.

The next ten years of my life were spent in Europe, and when I came home the recollection of Mrs. Amyot had become as inoffensive as one of those pathetic ghosts who are said to strive in vain to make themselves visible to the living. I did not even notice the fact that I no longer heard her spoken of; she had dropped like a dead leaf from the bough of memory.

A year or two after my return I was condemned to one of the worst punishments a worker can undergo — an enforced holiday. The doctors who pronounced the inhuman sentence decreed that it should be worked out in the South, and for a whole winter I carried my cough, my thermometer and my idleness from one fashionable orange grove to another. In the vast and melancholy sea of my disoccupation I clutched like a drowning man at any human driftwood within reach. I took a critical and depreciatory interest in the coughs, the thermometers and the idleness of my fellow sufferers; but to the healthy, the occupied, the transient I clung with undiscriminating enthusiasm.

In no other way can I explain, as I look back on it, the importance I attached to the leisurely confidences of a new arrival with a brown beard who, tilted back at my side on a hotel veranda hung with roses, imparted to me one afternoon the simple annals of his past. There was nothing in the tale to kindle the most inflammable imagination, and though the man had a pleasant frank face and a voice differing agreeably from the shrill inflections of our fellow lodgers, it is probable that under different conditions his discursive history of successful business ventures in a Western city would have affected me somewhat in the manner of a lullaby.

Even at the time I was not sure I liked his agreeable voice: it had a self-importance out of keeping with the humdrum nature of his story, as though a breeze engaged in shaking out a tablecloth should have fancied itself inflating a banner. But this criticism may have been a mere mark of my own fastidiousness, for the man seemed a simple fellow, satisfied with his middling fortunes, and already (he was not much past thirty) deep sunk in conjugal content.

He had just started on an anecdote connected with the cutting of his eldest boy's teeth, when a lady I knew, returning from her late drive, paused before us for a moment in the twilight, with the smile which is the feminine equivalent of beads to savages.

"Won't you take a ticket?" she said sweetly.

Of course I would take a ticket — but for what? I ventured to inquire.

The Pelican 55

"Oh, that's *so* good of you — for the lecture this evening. You needn't go, you know; we're none of us going; most of us have been through it already at Aiken and at Saint Augustine and at Palm Beach. I've given away my tickets to some new people who've just come from the North, and some of us are going to send our maids, just to fill up the room."

"And may I ask to whom you are going to pay this delicate attention?"

"Oh, I thought you knew — to poor Mrs. Amyot. She's been lecturing all over the South this winter; she's simply *haunted* me ever since I left New York — and we had six weeks of her at Bar Harbor last summer! One has to take tickets, you know, because she's a widow and does it for her son — to pay for his education. She's so plucky and nice about it, and talks about him in such a touching unaffected way, that everybody is sorry for her, and we all simply ruin ourselves in tickets. I do hope that boy's nearly educated!"

"Mrs. Amyot? Mrs. Amyot?" I repeated. "Is she *still* educating her son?"

"Oh, do you know about her? Has she been at it long? There's some comfort in that, for I suppose when the boy's provided for the poor thing will be able to take a rest — and give us one!"

She laughed and held out her hand.

"Here's your ticket. Did you say *tickets* — two? Oh, thanks. Of course you needn't go."

"But I mean to go. Mrs. Amyot is an old friend of mine."

"Do you really? That's awfully good of you. Perhaps I'll go too if I can persuade Charlie and the others to come. And I wonder" — in a well-directed aside — "if your friend — ?"

I telegraphed her under cover of the dusk that my friend was of too recent standing to be drawn into her charitable toils, and she masked her mistake under a rattle of friendly adjurations not to be late, and to be sure to keep a seat for her, as she had quite made up her mind to go even if Charlie and the others wouldn't.

The flutter of her skirts subsided in the distance, and my neighbor, who had half turned away to light a cigar, made no effort to reopen the conversation. At length, fearing he might have overheard the allusion to himself, I ventured to ask if he were going to the lecture that evening.

"Much obliged — I have a ticket," he said abruptly.

This struck me as in such bad taste that I made no answer; and it was he who spoke next.

"Did I understand you to say that you were an old friend of Mrs. Amyot's?"

"I think I may claim to be, if it is the same Mrs. Amyot I had the pleasure of knowing many years ago. My Mrs. Amyot used to lecture too — "

"To pay for her son's education?"

"I believe so."

"Well — see you later."

He got up and walked into the house.

In the hotel drawing room that evening there was but a meager sprinkling of guests, among whom I saw my brown-bearded friend sitting alone on a sofa, with his head against the wall. It could not have been curiosity to see Mrs. Amyot that had impelled him to attend the performance, for it would have been impossible for him, without changing his place, to command the improvised platform at the end of the room. When I looked at him he seemed lost in contemplation of the chandelier.

The lady from whom I had bought my tickets fluttered in late, unattended by Charlie and the others, and assuring me that she would *scream* if we had the lecture on Ibsen — she had heard it three times already that winter. A glance at the program reassured her: it informed us (in the lecturer's own slanting hand) that Mrs. Amyot was to lecture on the Cosmogony.

After a long pause, during which the small audience coughed and moved its chairs and showed signs of regretting that it had come, the door opened, and Mrs. Amyot stepped upon the platform. Ah, poor lady!

Someone said "Hush!" The coughing and chair shifting subsided, and she began.

It was like looking at one's self early in the morning in a cracked mirror. I had no idea I had grown so old. As for Lancelot, he must have a beard. A beard? The word struck me, and without knowing why I glanced across the room at my bearded friend on the sofa. Oddly enough he was looking at me, with a half-defiant, half-sullen expression; and as our glances crossed, and his fell, the conviction came to me that *he was Lancelot*.

I don't remember a word of the lecture; and yet there was enough of them to have filled a good-sized dictionary. The stream of Mrs. Amyot's eloquence had become a flood: one had the despairing sense that she had sprung a leak, and that until the plumber came there was nothing to be done about it.

The plumber came at length, in the shape of a clock striking ten; my companion, with a sigh of relief, drifted away in search of Charlie and the others; the audience scattered with the precipitation of people who had discharged a duty; and, without surprise, I found the brown-bearded stranger at my elbow.

We stood alone in the bare-floored room, under the flaring chandelier.

"I think you told me this afternoon that you were an old friend of Mrs. Amyot's?" he began awkwardly.

I assented.

"Will you come in and see her?"

"Now? I shall be very glad to, if—"

"She's ready; she's expecting you," he interposed.

He offered no further explanation, and I followed him in silence. He led me down the long corridor, and pushed open the door of a sitting room.

"Mother," he said, closing the door after we had entered, "here's the gentleman who says he used to know you."

Mrs. Amyot, who sat in an easy chair stirring a cup of bouillon, looked up with a start. She had evidently not seen me in the audience, and her son's description had failed to convey my identity. I saw a frightened look in her eyes; then, like a frost flower on a windowpane, the dimple expanded on her wrinkled cheek, and she held out her hand.

"I'm so glad," she said, "so glad!"

She turned to her son, who stood watching us. "You must have told Lancelot all about me—you've known me so long!"

"I haven't had time to talk to your son—since I knew he was your son," I explained.

Her brow cleared. "Then you haven't had time to say anything very dreadful?" she said with a laugh.

"It is he who has been saying dreadful things," I returned, trying to fall in with her tone.

I saw my mistake. "What things?" she faltered.

"Making me feel how old I am by telling me about his children."

"My grandchildren!" she exclaimed with a blush.

"Well, if you choose to put it so."

She laughed again, vaguely, and was silent. I hesitated a moment and then put out my hand.

"I see you are tired. I shouldn't have ventured to come in at this hour if your son—"

The son stepped between us. "Yes, I asked him to come," he said to his mother, in his clear self-assertive voice. "*I* haven't told him anything yet; but you've got to—now. That's what I brought him for."

His mother straightened herself, but I saw her eye waver.

"Lancelot—" she began.

"Mr. Amyot," I said, turning to the young man, "if your mother will let me come back tomorrow, I shall be very glad—"

He struck his hand hard against the table on which he was leaning.

"No, sir! It won't take long, but it's got to be said now."

He moved nearer to his mother, and I saw his lip twitch under his beard. After all, he was younger and less sure of himself than I had fancied.

"See here, Mother," he went on, "there's something here that's got to be cleared up, and as you say this gentleman is an old friend of yours it had better be cleared up in his presence. Maybe he can help explain it — and if he can't, it's got to be explained to *him*."

Mrs. Amyot's lips moved, but she made no sound. She glanced at me helplessly and sat down. My early inclination to thrash Lancelot was beginning to reassert itself. I took up my hat and moved toward the door.

"Mrs. Amyot is under no obligation to explain anything whatever to me," I said curtly.

"Well! She's under an obligation to me, then — to explain something in your presence." He turned to her again. "Do you know what the people in this hotel are saying? Do you know what he thinks — what they all think? That you're doing this lecturing to support me — to pay for my education! They say you go round telling them so. That's what they buy the tickets for — they do it out of charity. Ask him if it isn't what they say — ask him if they weren't joking about it on the piazza before dinner. The others think I'm a little boy, but he's known you for years, and he must have known how old I was. *He* must have known it wasn't to pay for my education!"

He stood before her with his hands clenched, the veins beating in his temples. She had grown very pale, and her cheeks looked hollow. When she spoke her voice had an odd click in it.

"If — if these ladies and gentlemen have been coming to my lectures out of charity, I see nothing to be ashamed of in that — " she faltered.

"If they've been coming out of charity to *me*," he retorted, "don't you see you've been making me a party to a fraud? Isn't there any shame in that?" His forehead reddened. "Mother! Can't you see the shame of letting people think I was a deadbeat, who sponged on you for my keep? Let alone making us both the laughingstock of every place you go to!"

"I never did that, Lancelot!"

"Did what?"

"Made you a laughingstock — "

He stepped close to her and caught her wrist.

"Will you look me in the face and swear you never told people you were doing this lecturing business to support me?"

There was a long silence. He dropped her wrists and she lifted a limp handkerchief to her frightened eyes. "I did do it — to support you — to educate you — " she sobbed.

"We're not talking about what you did when I was a boy. Everybody who knows me knows I've been a grateful son. Have I ever taken a penny from you since I left college ten years ago?"

"I never said you had! How can you accuse your mother of such wickedness, Lancelot?"

"Have you never told anybody in this hotel — or anywhere else in the last ten years — that you were lecturing to support me? Answer me that!"

"How can you," she wept, "before a stranger?"

"Haven't you said such things about *me* to strangers?" he retorted.

"Lancelot!"

"Well — answer me, then. Say you haven't, Mother!" His voice broke unexpectedly and he took her hand with a gentler touch. "I'll believe anything you tell me," he said almost humbly.

She mistook his tone and raised her head with a rash clutch at dignity.

"I think you'd better ask this gentleman to excuse you first."

"No, by God, I won't!" he cried. "This gentleman says he knows all about you and I mean him to know all about me, too. I don't mean that he or anybody else under this roof shall go on thinking for another twenty-four hours that a cent of their money has ever gone into my pockets since I was old enough to shift for myself. And he shan't leave this room till you've made that clear to him."

He stepped back as he spoke and put his shoulders against the door.

"My dear young gentleman," I said politely, "I shall leave this room exactly when I see fit to do so — and that is now. I have already told you that Mrs. Amyot owes me no explanation of her conduct."

"But I owe you an explanation of mine — you and everyone who has bought a single one of her lecture tickets. Do you suppose a man who's been through what I went through while that woman was talking to you in the porch before dinner is going to hold his tongue, and not attempt to justify himself? No decent man is going to sit down under that sort of thing. It's enough to ruin his character. If you're my mother's friend, you owe it to me to hear what I've got to say."

He pulled out his handkerchief and wiped his forehead.

"Good God, Mother!" he burst out suddenly, "what did you do it for? Haven't you had everything you wanted ever since I was able to pay for it? Haven't I paid you back every cent you spent on me when I was in college? Have I ever gone back on you since I was big enough to work?" He turned to me with a laugh. "I thought she did it to amuse herself — and because there was such a demand for her lectures. *Such a demand!* That's what she always told me. When we asked her to come out and spend this winter with us in Minneapolis, she wrote back that she couldn't because she had engagements all through the South, and her manager wouldn't let her off. That's the reason why I came all the way on here to see her. We thought she was the most popular lecturer in the United States, my wife and I did! We were awfully proud of it too, I can tell you." He dropped into a chair, still laughing.

"How can you, Lancelot, how can you!" His mother, forgetful of my presence, was clinging to him with tentative caresses. "When you didn't need the money any longer I spent it all on the children — you know I did."

"Yes, on lace christening dresses and life-size rocking horses with real manes! The kind of thing children can't do without."

"Oh, Lancelot, Lancelot — I loved them so! How can you believe such falsehoods about me?"

"What falsehoods about you?"

"That I ever told anybody such dreadful things?"

He put her back gently, keeping his eyes on hers. "Did you never tell anybody in this house that you were lecturing to support your son?"

Her hands dropped from his shoulders and she flashed round on me in sudden anger.

"I know what I think of people who call themselves friends and who come between a mother and her son!"

"Oh, Mother, Mother!" he groaned.

I went up to him and laid my hand on his shoulder.

"My dear man," I said, "don't you see the uselessness of prolonging this?"

"Yes, I do," he answered abruptly; and before I could forestall his movement he rose and walked out of the room.

There was a long silence, measured by the lessening reverberations of his footsteps down the wooden floor of the corridor.

When they ceased I approached Mrs. Amyot, who had sunk into her chair. I held out my hand and she took it without a trace of resentment on her ravaged face.

"I sent his wife a sealskin jacket at Christmas!" she said, with the tears running down her cheeks.

Souls Belated

I

THEIR RAILWAY carriage had been full when the train left Bologna; but at the first station beyond Milan their only remaining companion — a courtly person who ate garlic out of a carpetbag — had left his crumb-strewn seat with a bow.

Lydia's eye regretfully followed the shiny broadcloth of his retreating back till it lost itself in the cloud of touts and cab drivers hanging about the station; then she glanced across at Gannett and caught the same regret in his look. They were both sorry to be alone.

"*Par-ten-za!*" shouted the guard. The train vibrated to a sudden slamming of doors; a waiter ran along the platform with a tray of fossilized sandwiches; a belated porter flung a bundle of shawls and band-boxes into a third-class carriage; the guard snapped out a brief *Partenza!* which indicated the purely ornamental nature of his first shout; and the train swung out of the station.

The direction of the road had changed, and a shaft of sunlight struck across the dusty red-velvet seats into Lydia's corner. Gannett did not notice it. He had returned to his *Revue de Paris*, and she had to rise and lower the shade of the farther window. Against the vast horizon of their leisure such incidents stood out sharply.

Having lowered the shade, Lydia sat down, leaving the length of the carriage between herself and Gannett. At length he missed her and looked up.

"I moved out of the sun," she hastily explained.

He looked at her curiously: the sun was beating on her through the shade.

"Very well," he said pleasantly; adding, "You don't mind?" as he drew a cigarette case from his pocket.

It was a refreshing touch, relieving the tension of her spirit with the suggestion that, after all, if he could *smoke* — ! The relief was only

61

momentary. Her experience of smokers was limited (her husband had disapproved of the use of tobacco) but she knew from hearsay that men sometimes smoked to get away from things; that a cigar might be the masculine equivalent of darkened windows and a headache. Gannett, after a puff or two, returned to his review.

It was just as she had foreseen; he feared to speak as much as she did. It was one of the misfortunes of their situation that they were never busy enough to necessitate, or even to justify, the postponement of unpleasant discussions. If they avoided a question it was obviously, unconcealably because the question was disagreeable. They had unlimited leisure and an accumulation of mental energy to devote to any subject that presented itself; new topics were in fact at a premium. Lydia sometimes had premonitions of a famine-stricken period when there would be nothing left to talk about, and she had already caught herself doling out piecemeal what, in the first prodigality of their confidences, she would have flung to him in a breath. Their silence therefore might simply mean that they had nothing to say; but it was another disadvantage of their position that it allowed infinite opportunity for the classification of minute differences. Lydia had learned to distinguish between real and factitious silences; and under Gannett's she now detected a hum of speech to which her own thoughts made breathless answer.

How could it be otherwise, with that thing between them? She glanced up at the rack overhead. The *thing* was there, in her dressing bag, symbolically suspended over her head and his. He was thinking of it now, just as she was; they had been thinking of it in unison ever since they had entered the train. While the carriage had held other travelers they had screened her from his thoughts; but now that he and she were alone she knew exactly what was passing through his mind; she could almost hear him asking himself what he should say to her.

The thing had come that morning, brought up to her in an innocent-looking envelope with the rest of their letters, as they were leaving the hotel at Bologna. As she tore it open, she and Gannett were laughing over some ineptitude of the local guidebook — they had been driven, of late, to make the most of such incidental humors of travel. Even when she had unfolded the document she took it for some unimportant business paper sent abroad for her signature, and her eye traveled inattentively over the curly *Whereases* of the preamble until a word arrested her: Divorce. There it stood, an impassable barrier, between her husband's name and hers.

She had been prepared for it, of course, as healthy people are said to be prepared for death, in the sense of knowing it must come without in the least expecting that it will. She had known from the first that Tillotson meant to divorce her — but what did it matter? Nothing mattered, in those first days of supreme deliverance, but the fact that she was free; and not so much (she had begun to be aware) that freedom had released her from Tillotson as that it had given her to Gannett. This discovery had not been agreeable to her self-esteem. She had preferred to think that Tillotson had himself embodied all her reasons for leaving him; and those he represented had seemed cogent enough to stand in no need of reinforcement. Yet she had not left him till she met Gannett. It was her love for Gannett that had made life with Tillotson so poor and incomplete a business. If she had never, from the first, regarded her marriage as a full canceling of her claims upon life, she had at least, for a number of years, accepted it as a provisional compensation, — she had made it "do." Existence in the commodious Tillotson mansion in Fifth Avenue — with Mrs. Tillotson senior commanding the approaches from the second-story front windows — had been reduced to a series of purely automatic acts. The moral atmosphere of the Tillotson interior was as carefully screened and curtained as the house itself: Mrs. Tillotson senior dreaded ideas as much as a draft in her back. Prudent people liked an even temperature; and to do anything unexpected was as foolish as going out in the rain. One of the chief advantages of being rich was that one need not be exposed to unforeseen contingencies: by the use of ordinary firmness and common sense one could make sure of doing exactly the same thing every day at the same hour. These doctrines, reverentially imbibed with his mother's milk, Tillotson (a model son who had never given his parents an hour's anxiety) complacently expounded to his wife, testifying to his sense of their importance by the regularity with which he wore galoshes on damp days, his punctuality at meals, and his elaborate precautions against burglars and contagious diseases. Lydia, coming from a smaller town, and entering New York life through the portals of the Tillotson mansion, had mechanically accepted this point of view as inseparable from having a front pew in church and a parterre box at the opera. All the people who came to the house revolved in the same small circle of prejudices. It was the kind of society in which, after dinner, the ladies compared the exorbitant charges of their children's teachers, and agreed that, even with the new duties on French clothes, it was cheaper in the end to get everything from Worth; while the husbands, over their cigars, lamented municipal corruption, and decided that the men to start a reform were those who had no private interests at stake.

To Lydia this view of life had become a matter of course, just as lumbering about in her mother-in-law's landau had come to seem the only possible means of locomotion, and listening every Sunday to a fashionable Presbyterian divine the inevitable atonement for having thought oneself bored on the other six days of the week. Before she met Gannett her life had seemed merely dull; his coming made it appear like one of those dismal Cruikshank prints in which the people are all ugly and all engaged in occupations that are either vulgar or stupid.

It was natural that Tillotson should be the chief sufferer from this readjustment of focus. Gannett's nearness had made her husband ridiculous, and a part of the ridicule had been reflected on herself. Her tolerance laid her open to a suspicion of obtuseness from which she must, at all costs, clear herself in Gannett's eyes.

She did not understand this until afterwards. At the time she fancied that she had merely reached the limits of endurance. In so large a charter of liberties as the mere act of leaving Tillotson seemed to confer, the small question of divorce or no divorce did not count. It was when she saw that she had left her husband only to be with Gannett that she perceived the significance of anything affecting their relations. Her husband, in casting her off, had virtually flung her at Gannett: it was thus that the world viewed it. The measure of alacrity with which Gannett would receive her would be the subject of curious speculation over afternoon tea tables and in club corners. She knew what would be said — she had heard it so often of others! The recollection bathed her in misery. The men would probably back Gannett to "do the decent thing"; but the ladies' eyebrows would emphasize the worthlessness of such enforced fidelity; and after all, they would be right. She had put herself in a position where Gannett "owed" her something; where, as a gentleman, he was bound to "stand the damage." The idea of accepting such compensation had never crossed her mind; the so-called rehabilitation of such a marriage had always seemed to her the only real disgrace. What she dreaded was the necessity of having to explain herself; of having to combat his arguments; of calculating, in spite of herself, the exact measure of insistence with which he pressed them. She knew not whether she most shrank from his insisting too much or too little. In such a case the nicest sense of proportion might be at fault; and how easily to fall into the error of taking her resistance for a test of his sincerity! Whichever way she turned, an ironical implication confronted her: she had the exasperated sense of having walked into the trap of some stupid practical joke.

Beneath all these preoccupations lurked the dread of what he was thinking. Sooner or later, of course, he would have to speak; but that, in the meantime, he should think, even for a moment, that there was any use in speaking, seemed to her simply unendurable. Her sensitiveness on this point was aggravated by another fear, as yet barely on the level of consciousness; the fear of unwillingly involving Gannett in the trammels of her dependence. To look upon him as the instrument of her liberation; to resist in herself the least tendency to a wifely taking possession of his future; had seemed to Lydia the one way of maintaining the dignity of their relation. Her view had not changed, but she was aware of a growing inability to keep her thoughts fixed on the essential point — the point of parting with Gannett. It was easy to face as long as she kept it sufficiently far off: but what was this act of mental postponement but a gradual encroachment on his future? What was needful was the courage to recognize the moment when, by some word or look, their voluntary fellowship should be transformed into a bondage the more wearing that it was based on none of those common obligations which make the most imperfect marriage in some sort a center of gravity.

When the porter, at the next station, threw the door open, Lydia drew back, making way for the hoped-for intruder; but none came, and the train took up its leisurely progress through the spring wheat fields and budding copses. She now began to hope that Gannett would speak before the next station. She watched him furtively, half-disposed to return to the seat opposite his, but there was an artificiality about his absorption that restrained her. She had never before seen him read with so conspicuous an air of warding off interruption. What could he be thinking of? Why should he be afraid to speak? Or was it her answer that he dreaded?

The train paused for the passing of an express, and he put down his book and leaned out of the window. Presently he turned to her with a smile.

"There's a jolly old villa out here," he said.

His easy tone relieved her, and she smiled back at him as she crossed over to his corner.

Beyond the embankment, through the opening in a mossy wall, she caught sight of the villa, with its broken balustrades, its stagnant fountains, and the stone satyr closing the perspective of a dusky grass walk.

"How should you like to live there?" he asked as the train moved on.

"There?"

"In some such place, I mean. One might do worse, don't you think so? There must be at least two centuries of solitude under those yew trees. Shouldn't you like it?"

"I — I don't know," she faltered. She knew now that he meant to speak.

He lit another cigarette. "We shall have to live somewhere, you know," he said as he bent above the match.

Lydia tried to speak carelessly. "*Je n'en vois pas la nécessité!*[1] Why not live everywhere, as we have been doing?"

"But we can't travel forever, can we?"

"Oh, forever's a long word," she objected, picking up the review he had thrown aside.

"For the rest of our lives then," he said, moving nearer.

She made a slight gesture which caused his hand to slip from hers. "Why should we make plans? I thought you agreed with me that it's pleasanter to drift."

He looked at her hesitatingly. "It's been pleasant, certainly; but I suppose I shall have to get at my work again some day. You know I haven't written a line since — all this time," he hastily amended.

She flamed with sympathy and self-reproach. "Oh, if you mean *that* — if you want to write — of course we must settle down. How stupid of me not to have thought of it sooner! Where shall we go? Where do you think you could work best? We oughtn't to lose any more time."

He hesitated again. "I had thought of a villa in these parts. It's quiet; we shouldn't be bothered. Should you like it?"

"Of course I should like it." She paused and looked away. "But I thought — I remember your telling me once that your best work had been done in a crowd — in big cities. Why should you shut yourself up in a desert?"

Gannett, for a moment, made no reply. At length he said, avoiding her eye as carefully as she avoided his: "It might be different now; I can't tell, of course, till I try. A writer ought not to be dependent on his *milieu*; it's a mistake to humor oneself in that way; and I thought that just at first you might prefer to be — "

She faced him. "To be what?"

"Well — quiet. I mean — "

"What do you mean by 'at first'?" she interrupted.

He paused again. "I mean after we are married."

She thrust up her chin and turned toward the window. "Thank you!" she tossed back at him.

"Lydia!" he exclaimed blankly; and she felt in every fiber of her averted person that he had made the inconceivable, the unpardonable mistake of anticipating her acquiescence.

The train rattled on and he groped for a third cigarette. Lydia remained silent.

"I haven't offended you?" he ventured at length, in the tone of a man who feels his way.

1. *Je . . . nécessité!*] I don't see the need for it!

She shook her head with a sigh. "I thought you understood," she moaned. Their eyes met and she moved back to his side.

"Do you want to know how not to offend me? By taking it for granted, once for all, that you've said your say on the odious question and that I've said mine, and that we stand just where we did this morning before that—that hateful paper came to spoil everything between us!"

"To spoil everything between us? What on earth do you mean? Aren't you glad to be free?"

"I was free before."

"Not to marry me," he suggested.

"But I don't *want* to marry you!" she cried.

She saw that he turned pale. "I'm obtuse, I suppose," he said slowly. "I confess I don't see what you're driving at. Are you tired of the whole business? Or was I simply a—an excuse for getting away? Perhaps you didn't care to travel alone? Was that it? And now you want to chuck me?" His voice had grown harsh. "You owe me a straight answer, you know; don't be tenderhearted!"

Her eyes swam as she leaned to him. "Don't you see it's because I care—because I care so much? Oh, Ralph! Can't you see how it would humiliate me? Try to feel it as a woman would! Don't you see the misery of being made your wife in this way? If I'd known you as a girl—that would have been a real marriage! But now—this vulgar fraud upon society—and upon a society we despised and laughed at—this sneaking back into a position that we've voluntarily forfeited: don't you see what a cheap compromise it is? We neither of us believe in the abstract 'sacredness' of marriage; we both know that no ceremony is needed to consecrate our love for each other; what object can we have in marrying, except the secret fear of each that the other may escape, or the secret longing to work our way back gradually—oh, very gradually—into the esteem of the people whose conventional morality we have always ridiculed and hated? And the very fact that, after a decent interval, these same people would come and dine with us—the women who talk about the indissolubility of marriage, and who would let me die in a gutter today because I am 'leading a life of sin'—doesn't that disgust you more than their turning their backs on us now? I can stand being cut by them, but I couldn't stand their coming to call and asking what I meant to do about visiting that unfortunate Mrs. So-and-so!"

She paused, and Gannett maintained a perplexed silence.

"You judge things too theoretically," he said at length, slowly. "Life is made up of compromises."

"The life we ran away from—yes! If we had been willing to accept them" — she flushed — "we might have gone on meeting each other at Mrs. Tillotson's dinners."

He smiled slightly. "I didn't know that we ran away to found a new system of ethics. I supposed it was because we loved each other."

"Life is complex, of course; isn't it the very recognition of that fact that separates us from the people who see it *tout d'une pièce?*[2] If *they* are right — if marriage is sacred in itself and the individual must always be sacrificed to the family — then there can be no real marriage between us, since our — our being together is a protest against the sacrifice of the individual to the family." She interrupted herself with a laugh. "You'll say now that I'm giving you a lecture on sociology! Of course one acts as one can — as one must, perhaps — pulled by all sorts of invisible threads; but at least one needn't pretend, for social advantages, to subscribe to a creed that ignores the complexity of human motives — that classifies people by arbitrary signs, and puts it in everybody's reach to be on Mrs. Tillotson's visiting list. It may be necessary that the world should be ruled by conventions — but if we believed in them, why did we break through them? And if we don't believe in them, is it honest to take advantage of the protection they afford?"

Gannett hesitated. "One may believe in them or not; but as long as they do rule the world it is only by taking advantage of their protection that one can find a *modus vivendi.*"

"Do outlaws need a *modus vivendi?*"

He looked at her hopelessly. Nothing is more perplexing to man than the mental process of a woman who reasons her emotions.

She thought she had scored a point and followed it up passionately. "You do understand, don't you? You see how the very thought of the thing humiliates me! We are together today because we choose to be — don't let us look any farther than that!" She caught his hands. "*Promise* me you'll never speak of it again; promise me you'll never *think* of it even," she implored, with a tearful prodigality of italics.

Through what followed — his protests, his arguments, his final unconvinced submission to her wishes — she had a sense of his but half-discerning all that, for her, had made the moment so tumultuous. They had reached that memorable point in every heart history when, for the first time, the man seems obtuse and the woman irrational. It was the abundance of his intentions that consoled her, on reflection, for what they lacked in quality. After all, it would have been worse, incalculably worse, to have detected any overreadiness to understand her.

2. *tout d'une pièce*] all of a piece.

II

When the train at nightfall brought them to their journey's end at the edge of one of the lakes, Lydia was glad that they were not, as usual, to pass from one solitude to another. Their wanderings during the year had indeed been like the flight of outlaws: through Sicily, Dalmatia, Transylvania and Southern Italy they had persisted in their tacit avoidance of their kind. Isolation, at first, had deepened the flavor of their happiness, as night intensifies the scent of certain flowers; but in the new phase on which they were entering, Lydia's chief wish was that they should be less abnormally exposed to the action of each other's thoughts.

She shrank, nevertheless, as the brightly-looming bulk of the fashionable Anglo-American hotel on the water's brink began to radiate toward their advancing boat its vivid suggestion of social order, visitors' lists, Church services, and the bland inquisition of the *table d'hôte*. The mere fact that in a moment or two she must take her place on the hotel register as Mrs. Gannett seemed to weaken the springs of her resistance.

They had meant to stay for a night only, on their way to a lofty village among the glaciers of Monte Rosa; but after the first plunge into publicity, when they entered the dining room, Lydia felt the relief of being lost in a crowd, of ceasing for a moment to be the center of Gannett's scrutiny; and in his face she caught the reflection of her feeling. After dinner, when she went upstairs, he strolled into the smoking room, and an hour or two later, sitting in the darkness of her window, she heard his voice below and saw him walking up and down the terrace with a companion cigar at his side. When he came up he told her he had been talking to the hotel chaplain — a very good sort of fellow.

"Queer little microcosms, these hotels! Most of these people live here all summer and then migrate to Italy or the Riviera. The English are the only people who can lead that kind of life with dignity — those soft-voiced old ladies in Shetland shawls somehow carry the British Empire under their caps. *Civis Romanus sum.*[3] It's a curious study — there might be some good things to work up here."

---

3. *Civis Romanus sum.*] I am a Roman citizen. (This phrase, which proverbially made it safe for any Roman citizen to travel anywhere in his empire, is here applied to the British.)

He stood before her with the vivid preoccupied stare of the novelist on the trail of a "subject." With a relief that was half painful she noticed that, for the first time since they had been together, he was hardly aware of her presence.

"Do you think you could write here?"

"Here? I don't know." His stare dropped. "After being out of things so long one's first impressions are bound to be tremendously vivid, you know. I see a dozen threads already that one might follow —"

He broke off with a touch of embarrassment.

"Then follow them. We'll stay," she said with sudden decision.

"Stay here?" He glanced at her in surprise, and then, walking to the window, looked out upon the dusky slumber of the garden.

"Why not?" she said at length, in a tone of veiled irritation.

"The place is full of old cats in caps who gossip with the chaplain. Shall you like — I mean, it would be different if —"

She flamed up.

"Do you suppose I care? It's none of their business."

"Of course not; but you won't get them to think so."

"They may think what they please."

He looked at her doubtfully.

"It's for you to decide."

"We'll stay," she repeated.

Gannett, before they met, had made himself known as a successful writer of short stories and of a novel which had achieved the distinction of being widely discussed. The reviewers called him "promising," and Lydia now accused herself of having too long interfered with the fulfilment of his promise. There was a special irony in the fact, since his passionate assurances that only the stimulus of her companionship could bring out his latent faculty had almost given the dignity of a "vocation" to her course: there had been moments when she had felt unable to assume, before posterity, the responsibility of thwarting his career. And, after all, he had not written a line since they had been together: his first desire to write had come from renewed contact with the world! Was it all a mistake then? Must the most intelligent choice work more disastrously than the blundering combinations of chance? Or was there a still more humiliating answer to her perplexities? His sudden impulse of activity so exactly coincided with her own wish to withdraw, for a time, from the range of his observation, that she wondered if he too were not seeking sanctuary from intolerable problems.

"You must begin tomorrow!" she cried, hiding a tremor under the laugh with which she added, "I wonder if there's any ink in the inkstand?"

* * *

Whatever else they had at the Hotel Bellosguardo, they had, as Miss Pinsent said, "a certain tone." It was to Lady Susan Condit that they owed this inestimable benefit; an advantage ranking in Miss Pinsent's opinion above even the lawn tennis courts and the resident chaplain. It was the fact of Lady Susan's annual visit that made the hotel what it was. Miss Pinsent was certainly the last to underrate such a privilege: "It's so important, my dear, forming as we do a little family, that there should be someone to give *the tone*; and no one could do it better than Lady Susan — an earl's daughter and a person of such determination. Dear Mrs. Ainger now — who really *ought*, you know, when Lady Susan's away — absolutely refuses to assert herself." Miss Pinsent sniffed derisively. "A bishop's niece! — my dear, I saw her once actually give in to some South Americans — and before us all. She gave up her seat at table to oblige them — such a lack of dignity! Lady Susan spoke to her very plainly about it afterwards."

Miss Pinsent glanced across the lake and adjusted her auburn front.

"But of course I don't deny that the stand Lady Susan takes is not always easy to live up to — for the rest of us, I mean. Monsieur Grossart, our good proprietor, finds it trying at times, I know — he has said as much, privately, to Mrs. Ainger and me. After all, the poor man is not to blame for wanting to fill his hotel, is he? And Lady Susan is so difficult — so very difficult — about new people. One might almost say that she disapproves of them beforehand, on principle. And yet she's had warnings — she very nearly made a dreadful mistake once with the Duchess of Levens, who dyed her hair and — well, swore and smoked. One would have thought that might have been a lesson to Lady Susan." Miss Pinsent resumed her knitting with a sigh. "There are exceptions, of course. She took at once to you and Mr. Gannett — it was quite remarkable, really. Oh, I don't mean that either — of course not! It was perfectly natural — we *all* thought you so charming and interesting from the first day — we knew at once that Mr. Gannett was intellectual, by the magazines you took in; but you know what I mean. Lady Susan is so very — well, I won't say prejudiced, as Mrs. Ainger does — but so prepared *not* to like new people, that her taking to you in that way was a surprise to us all, I confess."

Miss Pinsent sent a significant glance down the long laurustinus alley from the other end of which two people — a lady and gentleman — were strolling toward them through the smiling neglect of the garden.

"In this case, of course, it's very different; that I'm willing to admit. Their looks are against them; but, as Mrs. Ainger says, one can't exactly tell them so."

"She's very handsome," Lydia ventured, with her eyes on the lady, who showed, under the dome of a vivid sunshade, the hourglass figure and superlative coloring of a Christmas chromo.

"That's the worst of it. She's too handsome."

"Well, after all, she can't help that."

"Other people manage to," said Miss Pinsent skeptically.

"But isn't it rather unfair of Lady Susan — considering that nothing is known about them?"

"But, my dear, that's the very thing that's against them. It's infinitely worse than any actual knowledge."

Lydia mentally agreed that, in the case of Mrs. Linton, it possibly might be.

"I wonder why they came here?" she mused.

"That's against them too. It's always a bad sign when loud people come to a quiet place. And they've brought van loads of boxes — her maid told Mrs. Ainger's that they meant to stop indefinitely."

"And Lady Susan actually turned her back on her in the salon?"

"My dear, she said it was for our sakes: that makes it so unanswerable! But poor Grossart *is* in a way! The Lintons have taken his most expensive suite, you know — the yellow damask drawing room above the portico — and they have champagne with every meal!"

They were silent as Mr. and Mrs. Linton sauntered by; the lady with tempestuous brows and challenging chin; the gentleman, a blond stripling, trailing after her, head downward, like a reluctant child dragged by his nurse.

"What does your husband think of them, my dear?" Miss Pinsent whispered as they passed out of earshot.

Lydia stooped to pick a violet in the border.

"He hasn't told me."

"Of your speaking to them, I mean. Would he approve of that? I know how very particular nice Americans are. I think your action might make a difference; it would certainly carry weight with Lady Susan."

"Dear Miss Pinsent, you flatter me!"

Lydia rose and gathered up her book and sunshade.

"Well, if you're asked for an opinion — if Lady Susan asks you for one — I think you ought to be prepared," Miss Pinsent admonished her as she moved away.

III

Lady Susan held her own. She ignored the Lintons, and her little family, as Miss Pinsent phrased it, followed suit. Even Mrs. Ainger agreed that it was obligatory. If Lady Susan owed it to the others not to speak to the Lintons, the others clearly owed it to Lady Susan to back her up. It was generally found expedient, at the Hotel Bellosguardo, to adopt this form of reasoning.

Whatever effect this combined action may have had upon the Lintons, it did not at least have that of driving them away. Monsieur Grossart, after a few days of suspense, had the satisfaction of seeing them settle down in his yellow damask *premier* with what looked like a permanent installation of palm trees and silk cushions, and a gratifying continuance in the consumption of champagne. Mrs. Linton trailed her Doucet draperies up and down the garden with the same challenging air, while her husband, smoking innumerable cigarettes, dragged himself dejectedly in her wake; but neither of them, after the first encounter with Lady Susan, made any attempt to extend their acquaintance. They simply ignored their ignorers. As Miss Pinsent resentfully observed, they behaved exactly as though the hotel were empty.

It was therefore a matter of surprise, as well as of displeasure, to Lydia, to find, on glancing up one day from her seat in the garden, that the shadow which had fallen across her book was that of the enigmatic Mrs. Linton.

"I want to speak to you," that lady said, in a rich hard voice that seemed the audible expression of her gown and her complexion.

Lydia started. She certainly did not want to speak to Mrs. Linton.

"Shall I sit down here?" the latter continued, fixing her intensely-shaded eyes on Lydia's face, "or are you afraid of being seen with me?"

"Afraid?" Lydia colored. "Sit down, please. What is it that you wish to say?"

Mrs. Linton, with a smile, drew up a garden chair and crossed one openwork ankle above the other.

"I want you to tell me what my husband said to your husband last night."

Lydia turned pale.

"My husband—to yours?" she faltered, staring at the other.

"Didn't you know they were closeted together for hours in the smoking-room after you went upstairs? My man didn't get to bed until nearly two o'clock and when he did I couldn't get a word out of him. When he wants to be aggravating I'll back him against anybody living!" Her teeth and eyes flashed persuasively upon Lydia. "But you'll tell me what they were talking about, won't you? I know I can trust you — you look so awfully kind. And it's for his own good. He's such a precious donkey and I'm so afraid he's got into some beastly scrape or other. If he'd only trust his own old woman! But they're always writing to him and setting him against me. And I've got nobody to turn to." She laid her hand on Lydia's with a rattle of bracelets. "You'll help me, won't you?"

Lydia drew back from the smiling fierceness of her brows.

"I'm sorry — but I don't think I understand. My husband has said nothing to me of — of yours."

The great black crescents above Mrs. Linton's eyes met angrily.

"I say — is that true?" she demanded.

Lydia rose from her seat.

"Oh, look here, I didn't mean that, you know — you mustn't take one up so! Can't you see how rattled I am?"

Lydia saw that, in fact, her beautiful mouth was quivering beneath softened eyes.

"I'm beside myself!" the splendid creature wailed, dropping into her seat.

"I'm so sorry," Lydia repeated, forcing herself to speak kindly; "but how can I help you?"

Mrs. Linton raised her head sharply.

"By finding out — there's a darling!"

"Finding what out?"

"What Trevenna told him."

"Trevenna — ?" Lydia echoed in bewilderment.

Mrs. Linton clapped her hand to her mouth.

"Oh, Lord — there, it's out! What a fool I am! But I supposed of course you knew; I supposed everybody knew." She dried her eyes and bridled. "Didn't you know that he's Lord Trevenna? I'm Mrs. Cope."

Lydia recognized the names. They had figured in a flamboyant elopement which had thrilled fashionable London some six months earlier.

"Now you see how it is — you understand, don't you?" Mrs. Cope continued on a note of appeal. "I knew you would — that's the reason I came to you. I suppose *he* felt the same thing about your husband; he's not spoken to another soul in the place." Her face grew anxious again. "He's awfully sensitive, generally — he feels our position, he says — as if it wasn't *my* place to feel that! But when he does get talking there's no knowing what he'll say. I know he's been brooding over something lately, and I *must* find out what it is — it's to his interest that I should. I always tell him that I think only of his interest; if he'd only trust me! But he's been so odd lately—I can't think what he's plotting. You will help me, dear?"

Lydia, who had remained standing, looked away uncomfortably.

"If you mean by finding out what Lord Trevenna has told my husband, I'm afraid it's impossible."

"Why impossible?"

"Because I infer that it was told in confidence."

Mrs. Cope stared incredulously.

"Well, what of that? Your husband looks such a dear—anyone can see he's awfully gone on you. What's to prevent your getting it out of him?"

Lydia flushed.

"I'm not a spy!" she exclaimed.

"A spy—a spy? How dare you?" Mrs. Cope flamed out. "Oh, I don't mean that either! Don't be angry with me—I'm so miserable." She essayed a softer note. "Do you call that spying—for one woman to help out another? I do need help so dreadfully! I'm at my wits' end with Trevenna, I am indeed. He's such a boy—a mere baby, you know; he's only two-and-twenty." She dropped her orbed lids. "He's younger than me—only fancy, a few months younger. I tell him he ought to listen to me as if I was his mother; oughtn't he now? But he won't, he won't! All his people are at him, you see—oh, I know *their* little game! Trying to get him away from me before I can get my divorce—that's what they're up to. At first he wouldn't listen to them; he used to toss their letters over to me to read; but now he reads them himself, and answers 'em too, I fancy; he's always shut up in his room, writing. If I only knew what his plan is I could stop him fast enough—he's such a simpleton. But he's dreadfully deep too—at times I can't make him out. But I know he's told your husband everything—I knew that last night the minute I laid eyes on him. And I *must* find out—you must help me—I've got no one else to turn to!"

She caught Lydia's fingers in a stormy pressure.

"Say you'll help me—you and your husband."

Lydia tried to free herself.

"What you ask is impossible; you must see that it is. No one could interfere in—in the way you ask."

Mrs. Cope's clutch tightened.

"You won't, then? You won't?"

"Certainly not. Let me go, please."

Mrs. Cope released her with a laugh.

"Oh, go by all means—pray don't let me detain you! Shall you go and tell Lady Susan Condit that there's a pair of us — or shall I save you the trouble of enlightening her?"

Lydia stood still in the middle of the path, seeing her antagonist through a mist of terror. Mrs. Cope was still laughing.

"Oh, I'm not spiteful by nature, my dear; but you're a little more than flesh and blood can stand! It's impossible, is it? Let you go, indeed! You're too good to be mixed up in my affairs, are you? Why, you little fool, the first day I laid eyes on you I saw that you and I were both in the same box — that's the reason I spoke to you."

She stepped nearer, her smile dilating on Lydia like a lamp through a fog.

"You can take your choice, you know; I always play fair. If you'll tell I'll promise not to. Now then, which is it to be?"

Lydia, involuntarily, had begun to move away from the pelting storm of words; but at this she turned and sat down again.

"You may go," she said simply. "I shall stay here."

IV

She stayed there for a long time, in the hypnotized contemplation, not of Mrs. Cope's present, but of her own past. Gannett, early that morning, had gone off on a long walk — he had fallen into the habit of taking these mountain tramps with various fellow lodgers; but even had he been within reach she could not have gone to him just then. She had to deal with herself first. She was surprised to find how, in the last months, she had lost the habit of introspection. Since their coming to the Hotel Bellosguardo she and Gannett had tacitly avoided themselves and each other.

She was aroused by the whistle of the three o'clock steamboat as it neared the landing just beyond the hotel gates. Three o'clock! Then Gannett would soon be back — he had told her to expect him before four. She rose hurriedly, her face averted from the inquisitorial façade of the hotel. She could not see him just yet; she could not go indoors. She slipped through one of the overgrown garden alleys and climbed a steep path to the hills.

It was dark when she opened their sitting-room door. Gannett was sitting on the window ledge smoking a cigarette. Cigarettes were now his chief resource: he had not written a line during the two months they had spent at the Hotel Bellosguardo. In that respect, it had turned out not to be the right *milieu* after all.

He started up at Lydia's entrance.

"Where have you been? I was getting anxious."

She sat down in a chair near the door.

"Up the mountain," she said wearily.

"Alone?"

"Yes."

Gannett threw away his cigarette: the sound of her voice made him want to see her face.

"Shall we have a little light?" he suggested.

She made no answer and he lifted the globe from the lamp and put a match to the wick. Then he looked at her.

"Anything wrong? You look done up."

She sat glancing vaguely about the little sitting room, dimly lit by the pallid-globed lamps, which left in twilight the outlines of the furniture, of his writing table heaped with books and papers, of the tea roses and jasmine drooping on the mantelpiece. How like home it had all grown — how like home!

"Lydia, what is wrong?" he repeated.

She moved away from him, feeling for her hatpins and turning to lay her hat and sunshade on the table.

Suddenly she said: "That woman has been talking to me."

Gannett stared.

"That woman? What woman?"

"Mrs. Linton — Mrs. Cope."

He gave a start of annoyance, still, as she perceived, not grasping the full import of her words.

"The deuce! She told you — ?"

"She told me everything."

Gannett looked at her anxiously.

"What impudence! I'm so sorry that you should have been exposed to this, dear."

"Exposed!" Lydia laughed.

Gannett's brow clouded and they looked away from each other.

"Do you know *why* she told me? She had the best of reasons. The first time she laid eyes on me she saw that we were both in the same box."

"Lydia!"

"So it was natural, of course, that she should turn to me in a difficulty."

"What difficulty?"

"It seems she has reason to think that Lord Trevenna's people are trying to get him away from her before she gets her divorce — "

"Well?"

"And she fancied he had been consulting with you last night as to — as to the best way of escaping from her."

Gannett stood up with an angry forehead.

"Well — what concern of yours was all this dirty business? Why should she go to you?"

"Don't you see? It's so simple. I was to wheedle his secret out of you."

"To oblige that woman?"

"Yes; or, if I was unwilling to oblige her, then to protect myself."

"To protect yourself? Against whom?"

"Against her telling everyone in the hotel that she and I are in the same box."

"She threatened that?"

"She left me the choice of telling it myself or of doing it for me."

"The beast!"

There was a long silence. Lydia had seated herself on the sofa, beyond the radius of the lamp, and he leaned against the window. His next question surprised her.

"When did this happen? At what time, I mean?"

She looked at him vaguely.

"I don't know — after luncheon, I think. Yes, I remember; it must have been at about three o'clock."

He stepped into the middle of the room and as he approached the light she saw that his brow had cleared.

"Why do you ask?" she said.

"Because when I came in, at about half-past three, the mail was just being distributed, and Mrs. Cope was waiting as usual to pounce on her letters; you know she was always watching for the postman. She was standing so close to me that I couldn't help seeing a big official-looking envelope that was handed to her. She tore it open, gave one look at the inside, and rushed off upstairs like a whirlwind, with the director shouting after her that she had left all her other letters behind. I don't believe she ever thought of you again after that paper was put into her hand."

"Why?"

"Because she was too busy. I was sitting in the window, watching for you, when the five o'clock boat left, and who should go on board, bag and baggage, valet and maid, dressing bags and poodle, but Mrs. Cope and Trevenna. Just an hour and a half to pack up in! And you should have seen her when they started. She was radiant — shaking hands with everybody — waving her handkerchief from the deck — distributing bows and smiles like an empress. If ever a woman got what she wanted just in the nick of time that woman did. She'll be Lady Trevenna within a week, I'll wager."

"You think she has her divorce?"

"I'm sure of it. And she must have got it just after her talk with you."

Lydia was silent.

At length she said, with a kind of reluctance, "She was horribly angry when she left me. It wouldn't have taken long to tell Lady Susan Condit."

"Lady Susan Condit has not been told."

"How do you know?"

"Because when I went downstairs half an hour ago I met Lady Susan on the way—"

He stopped, half smiling.

"Well?"

"And she stopped to ask if I thought you would act as patroness to a charity concert she is getting up."

In spite of themselves they both broke into a laugh. Lydia's ended in sobs and she sank down with her face hidden. Gannett bent over her, seeking her hands.

"That vile woman—I ought to have warned you to keep away from her; I can't forgive myself! But he spoke to me in confidence; and I never dreamed—well, it's all over now."

Lydia lifted her head.

"Not for me. It's only just beginning."

"What do you mean?"

She put him gently aside and moved in her turn to the window. Then she went on, with her face turned toward the shimmering blackness of the lake, "You see of course that it might happen again at any moment."

"What?"

"This—this risk of being found out. And we could hardly count again on such a lucky combination of chances, could we?"

He sat down with a groan.

Still keeping her face toward the darkness, she said, "I want you to go and tell Lady Susan—and the others."

Gannett, who had moved toward her, paused a few feet off.

"Why do you wish me to do this?" he said at length, with less surprise in his voice than she had been prepared for.

"Because I've behaved basely, abominably, since we came here: letting these people believe we were married—lying with every breath I drew—"

"Yes, I've felt that too," Gannett exclaimed with sudden energy.

The words shook her like a tempest: all her thoughts seemed to fall about her in ruins.

"You — you've felt so?"

"Of course I have." He spoke with low-voiced vehemence. "Do you suppose I like playing the sneak any better than you do? It's damnable."

He had dropped on the arm of a chair, and they stared at each other like blind people who suddenly see.

"But you have liked it here," she faltered.

"Oh, I've liked it — I've liked it." He moved impatiently. "Haven't you?"

"Yes," she burst out; "that's the worst of it — that's what I can't bear. I fancied it was for your sake that I insisted on staying — because you thought you could write here; and perhaps just at first that really was the reason. But afterwards I wanted to stay myself — I loved it." She broke into a laugh. "Oh, do you see the full derision of it? These people — the very prototypes of the bores you took me away from, with the same fenced-in view of life, the same keep-off-the-grass morality, the same little cautious virtues and the same little frightened vices — well, I've clung to them, I've delighted in them, I've done my best to please them. I've toadied Lady Susan, I've gossiped with Miss Pinsent, I've pretended to be shocked with Mrs. Ainger. Respectability! It was the one thing in life that I was sure I didn't care about, and it's grown so precious to me that I've stolen it because I couldn't get it in any other way."

She moved across the room and returned to his side with another laugh.

"I who used to fancy myself unconventional! I must have been born with a cardcase in my hand. You should have seen me with that poor woman in the garden. She came to me for help, poor creature, because she fancied that, having 'sinned,' as they call it, I might feel some pity for others who had been tempted in the same way. Not I! She didn't know me. Lady Susan would have been kinder, because Lady Susan wouldn't have been afraid. I hated the woman — my one thought was not to be seen with her — I could have killed her for guessing my secret. The one thing that mattered to me at that moment was my standing with Lady Susan!"

Gannett did not speak.

"And you — you've felt it too!" she broke out accusingly. "You've enjoyed being with these people as much as I have; you've let the chaplain talk to you by the hour about The Reign of Law and Professor Drummond. When they asked you to hand the plate in church I was watching you — *you wanted to accept.*"

She stepped close, laying her hand on his arm.

"Do you know, I begin to see what marriage is for. It's to keep people away from each other. Sometimes I think that two people who love each other can be saved from madness only by the things that come between them — children, duties, visits, bores, relations — the things that protect married people from each other. We've been too close together — that has been our sin. We've seen the nakedness of each other's souls."

She sank again on the sofa, hiding her face in her hands.

Gannett stood above her perplexedly: he felt as though she were being swept away by some implacable current while he stood helpless on its bank.

At length he said, "Lydia, don't think me a brute — but don't you see yourself that it won't do?"

"Yes, I see it won't do," she said without raising her head.

His face cleared.

"Then we'll go tomorrow."

"Go — where?"

"To Paris; to be married."

For a long time she made no answer; then she asked slowly, "Would they have us here if we were married?"

"Have us here?"

"I mean Lady Susan — and the others."

"Have us here? Of course they would."

"Not if they knew — at least, not unless they could pretend not to know."

He made an impatient gesture.

"We shouldn't come back here, of course; and other people needn't know — no one need know."

She sighed. "Then it's only another form of deception and a meaner one. Don't you see that?"

"I see that we're not accountable to any Lady Susans on earth!"

"Then why are you ashamed of what we are doing here?"

"Because I'm sick of pretending that you're my wife when you're not — when you won't be."

She looked at him sadly.

"If I were your wife you'd have to go on pretending. You'd have to pretend that I'd never been — anything else. And our friends would have to pretend that they believed what you pretended."

Gannett pulled off the sofa tassel and flung it away.

"You're impossible," he groaned.

"It's not I — it's our being together that's impossible. I only want you to see that marriage won't help it."

"What will help it then?"

She raised her head.

"My leaving you."

"Your leaving me?" He sat motionless, staring at the tassel which lay at the other end of the room. At length some impulse of retaliation for the pain she was inflicting made him say deliberately:

"And where would you go if you left me?"

"Oh!" she cried.

He was at her side in an instant.

"Lydia — Lydia — you know I didn't mean it; I couldn't mean it! But you've driven me out of my senses; I don't know what I'm saying. Can't you get out of this labyrinth of self-torture? It's destroying us both."

"That's why I must leave you."

"How easily you say it!" He drew her hands down and made her face him. "You're very scrupulous about yourself — and others. But have you thought of me? You have no right to leave me unless you've ceased to care —"

"It's because I care —"

"Then I have a right to be heard. If you love me you can't leave me." Her eyes defied him.

"Why not?"

He dropped her hands and rose from her side.

"Can you?" he said sadly.

The hour was late and the lamp flickered and sank. She stood up with a shiver and turned toward the door of her room.

V

At daylight a sound in Lydia's room woke Gannett from a troubled sleep. He sat up and listened. She was moving about softly, as though fearful of disturbing him. He heard her push back one of the creaking shutters; then there was a moment's silence, which seemed to indicate that she was waiting to see if the noise had roused him.

Presently she began to move again. She had spent a sleepless night, probably, and was dressing to go down to the garden for a breath of air. Gannett rose also; but some undefinable instinct made his movements as cautious as hers. He stole to his window and looked out through the slats of the shutter.

It had rained in the night and the dawn was gray and lifeless. The cloud-muffled hills across the lake were reflected in its surface as in a tarnished mirror. In the garden, the birds were beginning to shake the drops from the motionless laurustinus boughs.

An immense pity for Lydia filled Gannett's soul. Her seeming intellectual independence had blinded him for a time to the feminine cast of her mind. He had never thought of her as a woman who wept and clung: there was a lucidity in her intuitions that made them appear to be the result of reasoning. Now he saw the cruelty he had committed in detaching her from the normal conditions of life; he felt, too, the insight with which she had hit upon the real cause of their suffering. Their life was "impossible," as she had said — and its worse penalty was that it had made any other life impossible for them. Even had his love lessened, he was bound to her now by a hundred ties of pity and self-reproach; and she, poor child, must turn back to him as Latude returned to his cell.

A new sound startled him: it was the stealthy closing of Lydia's door. He crept to his own and heard her footsteps passing down the corridor. Then he went back to the window and looked out.

A minute or two later he saw her go down the steps of the porch and enter the garden. From his post of observation her face was invisible, but something about her appearance struck him. She wore a long traveling cloak and under its folds he detected the outline of a bag or bundle. He drew a deep breath and stood watching her.

She walked quickly down the laurustinus alley toward the gate; there she paused a moment, glancing about the little shady square. The stone benches under the trees were empty, and she seemed to gather resolution from the solitude about her, for she crossed the square to the steamboat landing, and he saw her pause before the ticket office at the head of the wharf. Now she was buying her ticket. Gannett turned his head a moment to look at the clock: the boat was due in five minutes. He had time to jump into his clothes and overtake her —

He made no attempt to move; an obscure reluctance restrained him. If any thought emerged from the tumult of his sensations, it was that he must let her go if she wished it. He had spoken last night of his rights: what were they? At the last issue, he and she were two separate beings, not made one by the miracle of common forbearances, duties, abnegations, but bound together in a *noyade* of passion that left them resisting yet clinging as they went down.

After buying her ticket, Lydia had stood for a moment looking out across the lake; then he saw her seat herself on one of the benches near the landing. He and she, at that moment, were both listening for the same sound: the whistle of the boat as it rounded the nearest promontory. Gannett turned again to glance at the clock: the boat was due now.

Where would she go? What would her life be when she had left him? She had no near relations and few friends. There was money enough . . . but she asked so much of life, in ways so complex and immaterial. He thought of her as walking barefooted through a stony waste. No one would understand her — no one would pity her — and he, who did both, was powerless to come to her aid.

He saw that she had risen from the bench and walked toward the edge of the lake. She stood looking in the direction from which the steamboat was to come; then she turned to the ticket office, doubtless to ask the cause of the delay. After that she went back to the bench and sat down with bent head. What was she thinking of?

The whistle sounded; she started up, and Gannett involuntarily made a movement toward the door. But he turned back and continued to watch her. She stood motionless, her eyes on the trail of smoke that preceded the appearance of the boat. Then the little craft rounded the point, a dead white object on the leaden water: a minute later it was puffing and backing at the wharf.

The few passengers who were waiting — two or three peasants and a snuffy priest — were clustered near the ticket office. Lydia stood apart under the trees.

The boat lay alongside now; the gangplank was run out and the peasants went on board with their baskets of vegetables, followed by the priest. Still Lydia did not move. A bell began to ring querulously; there was a shriek of steam, and someone must have called to her that she would be late, for she started forward, as though in answer to a summons. She moved waveringly, and at the edge of the wharf she paused. Gannett saw a sailor beckon to her; the bell rang again and she stepped upon the gangplank.

Halfway down the short incline to the deck she stopped again; then she turned and ran back to the land. The gangplank was drawn in, the bell ceased to ring, and the boat backed out into the lake. Lydia, with slow steps, was walking toward the garden.

As she approached the hotel she looked up furtively and Gannett drew back into the room. He sat down beside a table; a Bradshaw lay at his elbow, and mechanically, without knowing what he did, he began looking out the trains to Paris.

Xingu

I

MRS. BALLINGER is one of the ladies who pursue Culture in bands, as though it were dangerous to meet alone. To this end she had founded the Lunch Club, an association composed of herself and several other indomitable huntresses of erudition. The Lunch Club, after three or four winters of lunching and debate, had acquired such local distinction that the entertainment of distinguished strangers became one of its accepted functions; in recognition of which it duly extended to the celebrated Osric Dane, on the day of her arrival in Hillbridge, an invitation to be present at the next meeting.

The club was to meet at Mrs. Ballinger's. The other members, behind her back, were of one voice in deploring her unwillingness to cede her rights in favor of Mrs. Plinth, whose house made a more impressive setting for the entertainment of celebrities; while, as Mrs. Leveret observed, there was always the picture gallery to fall back on.

Mrs. Plinth made no secret of sharing this view. She had always regarded it as one of her obligations to entertain the Lunch Club's distinguished guests. Mrs. Plinth was almost as proud of her obligations as she was of her picture gallery; she was in fact fond of implying that the one possession implied the other, and that only a woman of her wealth could afford to live up to a standard as high as that which she had set herself. An all-round sense of duty, roughly adaptable to various ends, was, in her opinion, all that Providence exacted of the more humbly stationed; but the power which had predestined Mrs. Plinth to keep a footman clearly intended her to maintain an equally specialized staff of responsibilities. It was the more to be regretted that Mrs. Ballinger, whose obligations to society were bounded by the narrow scope of two parlormaids, should have been so tenacious of the right to entertain Osric Dane.

The question of that lady's reception had for a month past profoundly moved the members of the Lunch Club. It was not that they felt themselves unequal to the task, but that their sense of the opportunity plunged them into the agreeable uncertainty of the lady who weighs the alternatives of a well-stocked wardrobe. If such subsidiary members as Mrs. Leveret were fluttered by the thought of exchanging ideas with the author of *The Wings of Death,* no forebodings disturbed the conscious adequacy of Mrs. Plinth, Mrs. Ballinger and Miss Van Vluyck. *The Wings of Death* had, in fact, at Miss Van Vluyck's suggestion, been chosen as the subject of discussion at the last club meeting, and each member had thus been enabled to express her own opinion or to appropriate whatever sounded well in the comments of the others.

Mrs. Roby alone had abstained from profiting by the opportunity but it was now openly recognized that, as a member of the Lunch Club, Mrs. Roby was a failure. "It all comes," as Miss Van Vluyck put it, "of accepting a woman on a man's estimation." Mrs. Roby, returning to Hillbridge from a prolonged sojourn in exotic lands—the other ladies no longer took the trouble to remember where—had been heralded by the distinguished biologist, Professor Foreland, as the most agreeable woman he had ever met; and the members of the Lunch Club, impressed by an encomium that carried the weight of a diploma, and rashly assuming that the Professor's social sympathies would follow the line of his professional bent, had seized the chance of annexing a biological member. Their disillusionment was complete. At Miss Van Vluyck's first offhand mention of the pterodactyl Mrs. Roby had confusedly murmured: "I know so little about meters—" and after that painful betrayal of incompetence she had prudently withdrawn from further participation in the mental gymnastics of the club.

"I suppose she flattered him," Miss Van Vluyck summed up—"or else it's the way she does her hair."

The dimensions of Miss Van Vluyck's dining room having restricted the membership of the club to six, the nonconductiveness of one member was a serious obstacle to the exchange of ideas, and some wonder had already been expressed that Mrs. Roby should care to live, as it were, on the intellectual bounty of the others. This feeling was increased by the discovery that she had not yet read *The Wings of Death.* She owned to having heard the name of Osric Dane; but that—incredible as it appeared—was the extent of her acquaintance with the celebrated novelist. The ladies could not conceal their surprise; but Mrs. Ballinger, whose pride in the club made her wish to put even Mrs. Roby in the best possible light, gently insinuated that, though she had not had time to acquaint herself with *The Wings of Death,* she must at least be familiar with its equally remarkable predecessor, *The Supreme Instant.*

Mrs. Roby wrinkled her sunny brows in a conscientious effort of memory, as a result of which she recalled that, oh, yes, she *had* seen the book at her brother's, when she was staying with him in Brazil, and had even carried it off to read one day on a boating party; but they had all got to shying things at each other in the boat, and the book had gone overboard, so she had never had the chance —

The picture evoked by this anecdote did not increase Mrs. Roby's credit with the club, and there was a painful pause, which was broken by Mrs. Plinth's remarking: "I can understand that, with all your other pursuits, you should not find much time for reading; but I should have thought you might at least have *got up The Wings of Death* before Osric Dane's arrival."

Mrs. Roby took this rebuke good-humoredly. She had meant, she owned, to glance through the book; but she had been so absorbed in a novel of Trollope's that —

"No one reads Trollope now," Mrs. Ballinger interrupted.

Mrs. Roby looked pained. "I'm only just beginning," she confessed.

"And does he interest you?" Mrs. Plinth inquired.

"He amuses me."

"Amusement," said Mrs. Plinth, "is hardly what I look for in my choice of books."

"Oh, certainly, *The Wings of Death* is not amusing," ventured Mrs. Leveret, whose manner of putting forth an opinion was like that of an obliging salesman with a variety of other styles to submit if his first selection does not suit.

"Was it *meant* to be?" inquired Mrs. Plinth, who was fond of asking questions that she permitted no one but herself to answer. "Assuredly not."

"Assuredly not — that is what I was going to say," assented Mrs. Leveret, hastily rolling up her opinion and reaching for another. "It was meant to — to elevate."

Miss Van Vluyck adjusted her spectacles as though they were the black cap of condemnation. "I hardly see," she interposed, "how a book steeped in the bitterest pessimism can be said to elevate, however much it may instruct."

"I meant, of course, to instruct," said Mrs. Leveret, flurried by the unexpected distinction between two terms which she had supposed to be synonymous. Mrs. Leveret's enjoyment of the Lunch Club was frequently marred by such surprises; and not knowing her own value to the other ladies as a mirror for their mental complacency she was sometimes troubled by a doubt of her worthiness to join in their debates. It was only the fact of having a dull sister who thought her clever that saved her from a sense of hopeless inferiority.

"Do they get married in the end?" Mrs. Roby interposed.

"They—who?" the Lunch Club collectively exclaimed.

"Why, the girl and man. It's a novel, isn't it? I always think that's the one thing that matters. If they're parted it spoils my dinner."

Mrs. Plinth and Mrs. Ballinger exchanged scandalized glances, and the latter said: "I should hardly advise you to read *The Wings of Death* in that spirit. For my part, when there are so many books one *has* to read, I wonder how any one can find time for those that are merely amusing."

"The beautiful part of it," Laura Glyde murmured, "is surely just this—that no one can tell *how The Wings of Death* ends. Osric Dane, overcome by the awful significance of her own meaning, has mercifully veiled it—perhaps even from herself—as Apelles, in representing the sacrifice of Iphigenia, veiled the face of Agamemnon."

"What's that? It is poetry?" whispered Mrs. Leveret to Mrs. Plinth, who, disdaining a definite reply, said coldly: "You should look it up. I always make it a point to look things up." Her tone added—"Though I might easily have it done for me by the footman."

"I was about to say," Miss Van Vluyck resumed, "that it must always be a question whether a book *can* instruct unless it elevates."

"Oh—" murmured Mrs. Leveret, now feeling herself hopelessly astray.

"I don't know," said Mrs. Ballinger, scenting in Miss Van Vluyck's tone a tendency to depreciate the coveted distinction of entertaining Osric Dane; "I don't know that such a question can seriously be raised as to a book which has attracted more attention among thoughtful people than any novel since *Robert Elsmere*."

"Oh, but don't you see," exclaimed Laura Glyde, "that it's just the dark hopelessness of it all—the wonderful tone scheme of black on black—that makes it such an artistic achievement? It reminded me when I read it of Prince Rupert's *manière noire* . . . the book is etched, not painted, yet one feels the color values so intensely. . . ."

"Who is *he*?" Mrs. Leveret whispered to her neighbor. "Someone she's met abroad?"

"The wonderful part of the book," Mrs. Ballinger conceded, "is that it may be looked at from so many points of view. I hear that as a study of determinism Professor Lupton ranks it with *The Data of Ethics*."

"I'm told that Osric Dane spent ten years in preparatory studies before beginning to write it," said Mrs. Plinth. "She looks up everything—verifies everything. It has always been my principle, as you know. Nothing would induce me, now, to put aside a book before I'd finished it, just because I can buy as many more as I want."

"And what do *you* think of *The Wings of Death*?" Mrs. Roby abruptly asked her.

It was the kind of question that might be termed out of order, and the ladies glanced at each other as though disclaiming any share in such a breach of discipline. They all knew there was nothing Mrs. Plinth so much disliked as being asked her opinion of a book. Books were written to read; if one read them what more could be expected? To be questioned in detail regarding the contents of a volume seemed to her as great an outrage as being searched for smuggled laces at the Custom House. The club had always respected this idiosyncrasy of Mrs. Plinth's. Such opinions as she had were imposing and substantial: her mind, like her house, was furnished with monumental "pieces" that were not meant to be disarranged; and it was one of the unwritten rules of the Lunch Club that, within her own province, each member's habits of thought should be respected. The meeting therefore closed with an increased sense, on the part of the other ladies, of Mrs. Roby's hopeless unfitness to be one of them.

II

Mrs. Leveret, on the eventful day, arrived early at Mrs. Ballinger's, her volume of *Appropriate Allusions* in her pocket.

It always flustered Mrs. Leveret to be late at the Lunch Club: she liked to collect her thoughts and gather a hint, as the others assembled, of the turn the conversation was likely to take. Today, however, she felt herself completely at a loss; and even the familiar contact of *Appropriate Allusions*, which stuck into her as she sat down, failed to give her any reassurance. It was an admirable little volume, compiled to meet all the social emergencies; so that, whether on the occasion of Anniversaries, joyful or melancholy (as the classification ran), of Banquets, social or municipal, or of Baptisms, Church of England or sectarian, its student need never be at a loss for a pertinent reference. Mrs. Leveret, though she had for years devoutly conned its pages, valued it, however, rather for its moral support than for its practical services; for though in the privacy of her own room she commanded an army of quotations, these invariably deserted her at the critical moment, and the only phrase she retained — *Canst thou draw out leviathan with a hook?* — was one she had never yet found occasion to apply.

Today she felt that even the complete mastery of the volume would hardly have insured her self-possession; for she thought it probable that, even if she *did*, in some miraculous way, remember an Allusion, it would be only to find that Osric Dane used a different volume (Mrs. Leveret was convinced that literary people always carried them), and would consequently not recognize her quotations.

Mrs. Leveret's sense of being adrift was intensified by the appearance of Mrs. Ballinger's drawing room. To a careless eye its aspect was unchanged; but those acquainted with Mrs. Ballinger's way of arranging her books would instantly have detected the marks of recent perturbation. Mrs. Ballinger's province, as a member of the Lunch Club, was the Book of the Day. On that, whatever it was, from a novel to a treatise on experimental psychology, she was confidently, authoritatively "up." What became of last year's books, or last week's even; what she did with the "subjects" she had previously professed with equal authority; no one had ever yet discovered. Her mind was an hotel where facts came and went like transient lodgers, without leaving their address behind, and frequently without paying for their board. It was Mrs. Ballinger's boast that she was "abreast with the Thought of the Day," and her pride that this advanced position should be expressed by the books on her table. These volumes, frequently renewed, and almost always damp from the press, bore names generally unfamiliar to Mrs. Leveret, and giving her, as she furtively scanned them, a disheartening glimpse of new fields of knowledge to be breathlessly traversed in Mrs. Ballinger's wake. But today a number of maturer-looking volumes were adroitly mingled with the *primeurs* of the press — Karl Marx jostled Professor Bergson, and the *Confessions of St. Augustine* lay beside the last work on "Mendelism"; so that even to Mrs. Leveret's fluttered perceptions it was clear that Mrs. Ballinger didn't in the least know what Osric Dane was likely to talk about, and had taken measures to be prepared for anything. Mrs. Leveret felt like a passenger on an ocean steamer who is told that there is no immediate danger, but that she had better put on her lifebelt.

It was a relief to be roused from these forebodings by Miss Van Vluyck's arrival.

"Well, my dear," the newcomer briskly asked her hostess, "what subjects are we to discuss today?"

Mrs. Ballinger was furtively replacing a volume of Wordsworth by a copy of Verlaine. "I hardly know," she said, somewhat nervously. "Perhaps we had better leave that to circumstances."

"Circumstances?" said Miss Van Vluyck drily. "That means, I suppose, that Laura Glyde will take the floor as usual, and we shall be deluged with literature."

Philanthropy and statistics were Miss Van Vluyck's province, and she resented any tendency to divert their guest's attention from these topics.

Mrs. Plinth at this moment appeared.

"Literature?" she protested in a tone of remonstrance. "But this is perfectly unexpected. I understood we were to talk of Osric Dane's novel."

Mrs. Ballinger winced at the discrimination, but let it pass. "We can hardly make that our chief subject — at least not *too* intentionally," she suggested. "Of course we can let our talk *drift* in that direction; but we ought to have some other topic as an introduction, and that is what I wanted to consult you about. The fact is, we know so little of Osric Dane's taste and interests that it is difficult to make any special preparation."

"It may be difficult," said Mrs. Plinth with decision, "but it is necessary. I know what that happy-go-lucky principle leads to. As I told one of my nieces the other day, there are certain emergencies for which a lady should always be prepared. It's in shocking taste to wear colors when one pays a visit of condolence, or a last year's dress when there are reports that one's husband is on the wrong side of the market; and so it is with conversation. All I ask is that I should know beforehand what is to be talked about; then I feel sure of being able to say the proper thing."

"I quite agree with you," Mrs. Ballinger assented; "but — "

And at that instant, heralded by the fluttered parlormaid, Osric Dane appeared upon the threshold.

Mrs. Leveret told her sister afterward that she had known at a glance what was coming. She saw that Osric Dane was not going to meet them halfway. That distinguished personage had indeed entered with an air of compulsion not calculated to promote the easy exercise of hospitality. She looked as though she were about to be photographed for a new edition of her books.

The desire to propitiate a divinity is generally in inverse ratio to its responsiveness, and the sense of discouragement produced by Osric Dane's entrance visibly increased the Lunch Club's eagerness to please her. Any lingering idea that she might consider herself under an obligation to her entertainers was at once dispelled by her manner: as Mrs. Leveret said afterward to her sister, she had a way of looking at you that made you feel as if there was something wrong with your hat. This evidence of greatness produced such an immediate impression on the ladies that a shudder of awe ran through them when Mrs. Roby, as their hostess led the great personage into the dining room, turned back to whisper to the others: "What a brute she is!"

The hour about the table did not tend to revise this verdict. It was passed by Osric Dane in the silent deglutition of Mrs. Ballinger's menu, and by the members of the club in the emission of tentative platitudes which their guest seemed to swallow as perfunctorily as the successive courses of the luncheon.

Mrs. Ballinger's reluctance to fix a topic had thrown the club into a mental disarray which increased with the return to the drawing room, where the actual business of discussion was to open. Each lady waited for the other to speak; and there was a general shock of disappointment when their hostess opened the conversation by the painfully common-place inquiry: "Is this your first visit to Hillbridge?"

Even Mrs. Leveret was conscious that this was a bad beginning; and a vague impulse of deprecation made Miss Glyde interject: "It is a very small place indeed."

Mrs. Plinth bristled. "We have a great many representative people," she said, in the tone of one who speaks for her order.

Osric Dane turned to her. "What do they represent?" she asked.

Mrs. Plinth's constitutional dislike to being questioned was intensified by her sense of unpreparedness; and her reproachful glance passed the question on to Mrs. Ballinger.

"Why," said the lady, glancing in turn at the other members, "as a community I hope it is not too much to say that we stand for culture."

"For art—" Miss Glyde interjected.

"For art and literature," Mrs. Ballinger amended.

"And for sociology, I trust," snapped Miss Van Vluyck.

"We have a standard," said Mrs. Plinth, feeling herself suddenly secure on the vast expanse of a generalization; and Mrs. Leveret, thinking there must be room for more than one on so broad a statement, took courage to murmur: "Oh, certainly; we have a standard."

"The object of our little club," Mrs. Ballinger continued, "is to concentrate the highest tendencies of Hillbridge—to centralize and focus its intellectual effort."

This was felt to be so happy that the ladies drew an almost audible breath of relief.

"We aspire," the President went on, "to be in touch with whatever is highest in art, literature and ethics."

Osric Dane again turned to her. "What ethics?" she asked.

A tremor of apprehension encircled the room. None of the ladies required any preparation to pronounce on a question of morals; but when they were called ethics it was different. The club, when fresh from the *Encyclopedia Britannica*, the *Reader's Handbook* or Smith's *Classical Dictionary*, could deal confidently with any subject; but when taken unawares it had been known to define agnosticism as a heresy of the Early Church and Professor Froude as a distinguished histologist; and such minor members as Mrs. Leveret still secretly regarded ethics as something vaguely pagan.

Even to Mrs. Ballinger, Osric Dane's question was unsettling, and there was a general sense of gratitude when Laura Glyde leaned forward to say, with her most sympathetic accent: "You must excuse us, Mrs. Dane, for not being able, just at present, to talk of anything but *The Wings of Death*."

"Yes," said Miss Van Vluyck, with a sudden resolve to carry the war into the enemy's camp. "We are so anxious to know the exact purpose you had in mind in writing your wonderful book."

"You will find," Mrs. Plinth interposed, "that we are not superficial readers."

"We are eager to hear from you," Miss Van Vluyck continued, "if the pessimistic tendency of the book is an expression of your own convictions or —"

"Or merely," Miss Glyde thrust in, "a somber background brushed in to throw your figures into more vivid relief. *Are* you not primarily plastic?"

"*I* have always maintained," Mrs. Ballinger interposed, "that you represent the purely objective method —"

Osric Dane helped herself critically to coffee. "How do you define objective?" she then inquired.

There was a flurried pause before Laura Glyde intensely murmured: "In reading *you* we don't define, we feel."

Osric Dane smiled. "The cerebellum," she remarked, "is not infrequently the seat of the literary emotions." And she took a second lump of sugar.

The sting that this remark was vaguely felt to conceal was almost neutralized by the satisfaction of being addressed in such technical language.

"Ah, the cerebellum," said Mrs. Van Vluyck complacently. "The club took a course in psychology last winter."

"Which psychology?" asked Osric Dane.

There was an agonizing pause, during which each member of the club secretly deplored the distressing inefficiency of the others. Only Mrs. Roby went on placidly sipping her chartreuse. At last Mrs. Ballinger said, with an attempt at a high tone: "Well, really, you know, it was last year that we took psychology, and this winter we have been so absorbed in —"

She broke off, nervously trying to recall some of the club's discussions; but her faculties seemed to be paralyzed by the petrifying stare of Osric Dane. What *had* the club been absorbed in? Mrs. Ballinger, with a vague purpose of gaining time, repeated slowly: "We've been so intensely absorbed in —"

Mrs. Roby put down her liqueur glass and drew near the group with a smile.

"In Xingu?" she gently prompted.

A thrill ran through the other members. They exchanged confused glances, and then, with one accord, turned a gaze of mingled relief and interrogation on their rescuer. The expression of each denoted a different phase of the same emotion. Mrs. Plinth was the first to compose her features to an air of reassurance: after a moment's hasty adjustment her look almost implied that it was she who had given the word to Mrs. Ballinger.

"Xingu, of course!" exclaimed the latter with her accustomed promptness, while Miss Van Vluyck and Laura Glyde seemed to be plumbing the depths of memory, and Mrs. Leveret, feeling apprehensively for *Appropriate Allusions*, was somehow reassured by the uncomfortable pressure of its bulk against her person.

Osric Dane's change of countenance was no less striking than that of her entertainers. She too put down her coffee cup, but with a look of distinct annoyance; she too wore, for a brief moment, what Mrs. Roby afterward described as the look of feeling for something in the back of her head; and before she could dissemble these momentary signs of weakness, Mrs. Roby, turning to her with a deferential smile, had said: "And we've been so hoping that today you would tell us just what you think of it."

Osric Dane received the homage of the smile as a matter of course; but the accompanying question obviously embarrassed her, and it became clear to her observers that she was not quick at shifting her facial scenery. It was as though her countenance had so long been set in an expression of unchallenged superiority that the muscles had stiffened, and refused to obey her orders.

"Xingu —" she said, as if seeking in her turn to gain time.

Mrs. Roby continued to press her. "Knowing how engrossing the subject is, you will understand how it happens that the club has let everything else go to the wall for the moment. Since we took up Xingu I might almost say — were it not for your books — that nothing else seems to us worth remembering."

Osric Dane's stern features were darkened rather than lit up by an uneasy smile. "I am glad to hear that you make one exception," she gave out between narrowed lips.

"Oh, of course," Mrs. Roby said prettily; "but as you have shown us that — so very naturally! — you don't care to talk of your own things, we really can't let you off from telling us exactly what you think about Xingu; especially," she added, with a still more persuasive smile, "as some people say that one of your last books was saturated with it."

It was an *it*, then — the assurance sped like fire through the parched minds of the other members. In their eagerness to gain the least little clue to Xingu they almost forgot the joy of assisting at the discomfiture of Mrs. Dane.

The latter reddened nervously under her antagonist's challenge. "May I ask," she faltered out, "to which of my books you refer?"

Mrs. Roby did not falter. "That's just what I want you to tell us; because, though I was present, I didn't actually take part."

"Present at what?" Mrs. Dane took her up; and for an instant the trembling members of the Lunch Club thought that the champion Providence had raised up for them had lost a point. But Mrs. Roby explained herself gaily: "At the discussion, of course. And so we're dreadfully anxious to know just how it was that you went into the Xingu."

There was a portentous pause, a silence so big with incalculable dangers that the members with one accord checked the words on their lips, like soldiers dropping their arms to watch a single combat between their leaders. Then Mrs. Dane gave expression to their inmost dread by saying sharply: "Ah — you say *the* Xingu, do you?"

Mrs. Roby smiled undauntedly. "It *is* a shade pedantic, isn't it? Personally, I always drop the article: but I don't know how the other members feel about it."

The other members looked as though they would willingly have dispensed with this appeal to their opinion, and Mrs. Roby, after a bright glance about the group, went on: "They probably think, as I do, that nothing really matters except the thing itself — except Xingu."

No immediate reply seemed to occur to Mrs. Dane, and Mrs. Ballinger gathered courage to say: "Surely everyone must feel that about Xingu."

Mrs. Plinth came to her support with a heavy murmur of assent, and Laura Glyde sighed out emotionally: "I have known cases where it has changed a whole life."

"It has done me worlds of good," Mrs. Leveret interjected, seeming to herself to remember that she had either taken it or read it the winter before.

"Of course," Mrs. Roby admitted, "the difficulty is that one must give up so much time to it. It's very long."

"I can't imagine," said Miss Van Vluyck, "grudging the time given to such a subject."

"And deep in places," Mrs. Roby pursued; (so then it was a book!) "And it isn't easy to skip."

"I never skip," said Mrs. Plinth dogmatically.

"Ah, it's dangerous to, in Xingu. Even at the start there are places where one can't. One must just wade through."

"I should hardly call it *wading*," said Mrs. Ballinger sarcastically.

Mrs. Roby sent her a look of interest. "Ah — you always found it went swimmingly?"

Mrs. Ballinger hesitated. "Of course there are difficult passages," she conceded.

"Yes; some are not at all clear — even," Mrs. Roby added, "if one is familiar with the original."

"As I suppose you are?" Osric Dane interposed, suddenly fixing her with a look of challenge.

Mrs. Roby met it by a deprecating gesture. "Oh, it's really not difficult up to a certain point; though some of the branches are very little known, and it's almost impossible to get at the source."

"Have you ever tried?" Mrs. Plinth inquired, still distrustful of Mrs. Roby's thoroughness.

Mrs. Roby was silent for a moment; then she replied with lowered lids: "No — but a friend of mine did; a very brilliant man; and he told me it was best for women — not to. . . ."

A shudder ran around the room. Mrs. Leveret coughed so that the parlormaid, who was handing the cigarettes, should not hear; Miss Van Vluyck's face took on a nauseated expression, and Mrs. Plinth looked as if she were passing someone she did not care to bow to. But the most remarkable result of Mrs. Roby's words was the effect they produced on the Lunch Club's distinguished guest. Osric Dane's impassive features suddenly softened to an expression of the warmest human sympathy, and edging her chair toward Mrs. Roby's she asked: "Did he really? And — did you find he was right?"

Mrs. Ballinger, in whom annoyance at Mrs. Roby's unwonted assumption of prominence was beginning to displace gratitude for the aid she had rendered, could not consent to her being allowed, by such dubious means, to monopolize the attention of their guest. If Osric Dane had not enough self-respect to resent Mrs. Roby's flippancy, at least the Lunch Club would do so in the person of its President.

Mrs. Ballinger laid her hand on Mrs. Roby's arm. "We must not forget," she said with a frigid amiability, "that absorbing as Xingu is to *us*, it may be less interesting to —"

"Oh, no, on the contrary, I assure you," Osric Dane intervened.

" — to others," Mrs. Ballinger finished firmly; "and we must not allow
ır little meeting to end without persuading Mrs. Dane to say a few
ords to us on a subject which, today, is much more present in all our
oughts. I refer, of course, to *The Wings of Death*."

The other members, animated by various degrees of the same senti-
ent, and encouraged by the humanized mien of their redoubtable
ıest, repeated after Mrs. Ballinger: "Oh, yes, you really *must* talk to us a
tle about your book."

Osric Dane's expression became as bored, though not as haughty, as
ıen her work had been previously mentioned. But before she could
spond to Mrs. Ballinger's request, Mrs. Roby had risen from her seat,
ıd was pulling down her veil over her frivolous nose.

"I'm so sorry," she said, advancing toward her hostess with out-
etched hand, "but before Mrs. Dane begins I think I'd better run
·ay. Unluckily, as you know, I haven't read her books, so I should be at
errible disadvantage among you all, and besides, I've an engagement
play bridge."

If Mrs. Roby had simply pleaded her ignorance of Osric Dane's works
a reason for withdrawing, the Lunch Club, in view of her recent
owess, might have approved such evidence of discretion; but to couple
is excuse with the brazen announcement that she was foregoing the
ivilege for the purpose of joining a bridge party was only one more
stance of her deplorable lack of discrimination.

The ladies were disposed, however, to feel that her departure — now
at she had performed the sole service she was ever likely to render
em — would probably make for greater order and dignity in the im-
nding discussion, besides relieving them of the sense of self-distrust
ıich her presence always mysteriously produced. Mrs. Ballinger there-
·e restricted herself to a formal murmur of regret, and the other
embers were just grouping themselves comfortably about Osric Dane
ıen the latter, to their dismay, started up from the sofa on which she
d been seated.

"Oh wait — do wait, and I'll go with you!" she called out to Mrs. Roby;
d, seizing the hands of the disconcerted members, she administered a
:ies of farewell pressures with the mechanical haste of a railway
nductor punching tickets.

"I'm so sorry — I'd quite forgotten — " she flung back at them from the
reshold; and as she joined Mrs. Roby, who had turned in surprise at
r appeal, the other ladies had the mortification of hearing her say, in a
ice which she did not take the pains to lower: "If you'll let me walk a
:le way with you, I should so like to ask you a few more questions about
ıgu. . . ."

III

The incident had been so rapid that the door closed on the departir pair before the other members had time to understand what was ha pening. Then a sense of the indignity put upon them by Osric Dane unceremonious desertion began to contend with the confused feelir that they had been cheated out of their due without exactly knowir how or why.

There was a silence, during which Mrs. Ballinger, with a perfuncto hand, rearranged the skillfully grouped literature at which her disti guished guest had not so much as glanced; then Miss Van Vluyck tart pronounced: "Well, I can't say that I consider Osric Dane's departure great loss."

This confession crystallized the resentment of the other members, ar Mrs. Leveret exclaimed: "I do believe she came on purpose to be nasty

It was Mrs. Plinth's private opinion that Osric Dane's attitude towa the Lunch Club might have been very different had it welcomed her the majestic setting of the Plinth drawing rooms; but not liking to refle on the inadequacy of Mrs. Ballinger's establishment she sought a roun about satisfaction in deprecating her lack of foresight.

"I said from the first that we ought to have had a subject ready. I what always happens when you're unprepared. Now if we'd only got Xingu—"

The slowness of Mrs. Plinth's mental processes was always allowed f by the club; but this instance of it was too much for Mrs. Ballinge equanimity.

"Xingu!" she scoffed. "Why, it was the fact of our knowing so mu more about it than she did—unprepared though we were—that mac Osric Dane so furious. I should have thought that was plain enough everybody!"

This retort impressed even Mrs. Plinth, and Laura Glyde, moved an impulse of generosity, said: "Yes, we really ought to be grateful Mrs. Roby for introducing the topic. It may have made Osric Dar furious, but at least it made her civil."

"I am glad we were able to show her," added Miss Van Vluyck, "tha broad and up-to-date culture is not confined to the great intellectu centers."

This increased the satisfaction of the other members, and they beg; to forget their wrath against Osric Dane in the pleasure of havir contributed to her discomfiture.

Miss Van Vluyck thoughtfully rubbed her spectacles. "What surprised me most," she continued, "was that Fanny Roby should be so up on Xingu."

This remark threw a slight chill on the company, but Mrs. Ballinger said with an air of indulgent irony: "Mrs. Roby always has the knack of making a little go a long way; still, we certainly owe her a debt for happening to remember that she'd heard of Xingu." And this was felt by the other members to be a graceful way of canceling once and for all the club's obligation to Mrs. Roby.

Even Mrs. Leveret took courage to speed a timid shaft of irony. "I fancy Osric Dane hardly expected to take a lesson in Xingu at Hillbridge!"

Mrs. Ballinger smiled. "When she asked me what we represented — do you remember? — I wish I'd simply said we represented Xingu!"

All the ladies laughed appreciatively at this sally, except Mrs. Plinth, who said, after a moment's deliberation: "I'm not sure it would have been wise to do so."

Mrs. Ballinger, who was already beginning to feel as if she had launched at Osric Dane the retort which had just occurred to her, turned ironically on Mrs. Plinth. "May I ask why?" she inquired.

Mrs. Plinth looked grave. "Surely," she said, "I understood from Mrs. Roby herself that the subject was one it was as well not to go into too deeply?"

Miss Van Vluyck rejoined with precision: "I think that applied only to an investigation of the origin of the — of the — "; and suddenly she found that her usually accurate memory had failed her. "It's a part of the subject I never studied myself," she concluded.

"Nor I," said Mrs. Ballinger.

Laura Glyde bent toward them with widened eyes. "And yet it seems — doesn't it — the part that is fullest of an esoteric fascination?"

"I don't know on what you base that," said Miss Van Vluyck argumentatively.

"Well, didn't you notice how intensely interested Osric Dane became as soon as she heard what the brilliant foreigner — he *was* a foreigner, wasn't he — had told Mrs. Roby about the origin — the origin of the rite — or whatever you call it?"

Mrs. Plinth looked disapproving, and Mrs. Ballinger visibly wavered. Then she said: "It may not be desirable to touch on the — on that part of the subject in general conversation; but, from the importance it evidently has to a woman of Osric Dane's distinction, I feel as if we ought not to be afraid to discuss it among ourselves — without gloves — though with closed doors, if necessary."

"I'm quite of your opinion," Miss Van Vluyck came briskly to her support; "on condition, that is, that all grossness of language is avoided."

"Oh, I'm sure we shall understand without that," Mrs. Leveret tittered; and Laura Glyde added significantly: "I fancy we can read between the lines," while Mrs. Ballinger rose to assure herself that the doors were really closed.

Mrs. Plinth had not yet given her adhesion. "I hardly see," she began, "what benefit is to be derived from investigating such peculiar customs—"

But Mrs. Ballinger's patience had reached the extreme limit of tension. "This at least," she returned; "that we shall not be placed again in the humiliating position of finding ourselves less up on our own subjects than Fanny Roby!"

Even to Mrs. Plinth this argument was conclusive. She peered furtively about the room and lowered her commanding tones to ask: "Have you got a copy?"

"A—a copy?" stammered Mrs. Ballinger. She was aware that the other members were looking at her expectantly, and that this answer was inadequate, so she supported it by asking another question. "A copy of what?"

Her companions bent their expectant gaze on Mrs. Plinth, who, in turn, appeared less sure of herself than usual. "Why, of—of—the book," she explained.

"What book?" snapped Miss Van Vluyck, almost as sharply as Osric Dane.

Mrs. Ballinger looked at Laura Glyde, whose eyes were interrogatively fixed on Mrs. Leveret. The fact of being deferred to was so new to the latter that it filled her with an insane temerity. "Why, Xingu, of course!" she exclaimed.

A profound silence followed this challenge to the resources of Mrs. Ballinger's library, and the latter, after glancing nervously toward the Books of the Day, returned with dignity: "It's not a thing one cares to leave about."

"I should think *not!*" exclaimed Mrs. Plinth.

"It *is* a book, then?" said Miss Van Vluyck.

This again threw the company into disarray, and Mrs. Ballinger, with an impatient sigh, rejoined: "Why—there *is* a book—naturally. . . ."

"Then why did Miss Glyde call it a religion?"

Laura Glyde started up. "A religion? I never—"

"Yes, you did," Miss Van Vluyck insisted; "you spoke of rites; and Mrs. Plinth said it was a custom."

Miss Glyde was evidently making a desperate effort to recall her statement; but accuracy of detail was not her strongest point. At length she began in a deep murmur: "Surely they used to do something of the kind at the Eleusinian mysteries—"

"Oh—" said Miss Van Vluyck, on the verge of disapproval; and Mrs. Plinth protested: "I understood there was to be no indelicacy!"

Mrs. Ballinger could not control her irritation. "Really, it is too bad that we should not be able to talk the matter over quietly among ourselves. Personally, I think that if one goes into Xingu at all—"

"Oh, so do I!" cried Miss Glyde.

"And I don't see how one can avoid doing so, if one wishes to keep up with the Thought of the Day—"

Mrs. Leveret uttered an exclamation of relief. "There—that's it!" she interposed.

"What's it?" the President took her up.

"Why—it's a—a Thought: I mean a philosophy."

This seemed to bring a certain relief to Mrs. Ballinger and Laura Glyde, but Miss Van Vluyck said: "Excuse me if I tell you that you're all mistaken. Xingu happens to be a language."

"A language!" the Lunch Club cried.

"Certainly. Don't you remember Fanny Roby's saying that there were several branches, and that some were hard to trace? What could that apply to but dialects?"

Mrs. Ballinger could no longer restrain a contemptuous laugh. "Really, if the Lunch Club has reached such a pass that it has to go to Fanny Roby for instruction on a subject like Xingu, it had almost better cease to exist!"

"It's really her fault for not being clearer," Laura Glyde put in.

"Oh, clearness and Fanny Roby!" Mrs. Ballinger shrugged. "I dare say we shall find she was mistaken on almost every point."

"Why not look it up?" said Mrs. Plinth.

As a rule this recurrent suggestion of Mrs. Plinth's was ignored in the heat of discussion, and only resorted to afterward in the privacy of each member's home. But on the present occasion the desire to ascribe their own confusion of thought to the vague and contradictory nature of Mrs. Roby's statements caused the members of the Lunch Club to utter a collective demand for a book of reference.

At this point the production of her treasured volume gave Mrs. Leveret, for a moment, the unusual experience of occupying the center front; but she was not able to hold it long, for *Appropriate Allusions* contained no mention of Xingu.

"Oh, that's not the kind of thing we want!" exclaimed Miss Van Vluyck. She cast a disparaging glance over Mrs. Ballinger's assortment of literature, and added impatiently: "Haven't you any useful books?"

"Of course I have," replied Mrs. Ballinger indignantly; "I keep them in my husband's dressing room."

From this region, after some difficulty and delay, the parlormaid produced the W-Z volume of an *Encyclopedia* and, in deference to the fact that the demand for it had come from Miss Van Vluyck, laid the ponderous tome before her.

There was a moment of painful suspense while Miss Van Vluyck rubbed her spectacles, adjusted them, and turned to Z; and a murmur of surprise when she said: "It isn't here."

"I suppose," said Mrs. Plinth, "it's not fit to be put in a book of reference."

"Oh, nonsense!" exclaimed Mrs. Ballinger. "Try X."

Miss Van Vluyck turned back through the volume, peering short-sightedly up and down the pages, till she came to a stop and remained motionless, like a dog on a point.

"Well, have you found it?" Mrs. Ballinger inquired after a consider-able delay.

"Yes. I've found it," said Miss Van Vluyck in a queer voice.

Mrs. Plinth hastily interposed: "I beg you won't read it aloud if there's anything offensive."

Miss Van Vluyck, without answering, continued her silent scrutiny.

"Well, what *is* it?" exclaimed Laura Glyde excitedly.

"*Do* tell us!" urged Mrs. Leveret, feeling that she would have some-thing awful to tell her sister.

Miss Van Vluyck pushed the volume aside and turned slowly toward the expectant group.

"It's a river."

"A *river?*"

"Yes: in Brazil. Isn't that where she's been living?"

"Who? Fanny Roby? Oh, but you must be mistaken. You've been reading the wrong thing," Mrs. Ballinger exclaimed, leaning over her to seize the volume.

"It's the only Xingu in the *Encyclopedia*; and she *has* been living in Brazil," Miss Van Vluyck persisted.

"Yes: her brother has a consulship there," Mrs. Leveret interposed.

"But it's too ridiculous! I—we—why we *all* remember studying Xingu last year—or the year before last," Mrs. Ballinger stammered.

"I thought I did when *you* said so," Laura Glyde avowed.

"*I* said so?" cried Mrs. Ballinger.

"Yes. You said it had crowded everything else out of your mind."

"Well *you* said it had changed your whole life!"

"For that matter Miss Van Vluyck said she had never grudged the time she'd given it."

Mrs. Plinth interposed: "I made it clear that I knew nothing whatever of the original."

Mrs. Ballinger broke off the dispute with a groan. "Oh, what does it all matter if she's been making fools of us? I believe Miss Van Vluyck's right — she was talking of the river all the while!"

"How could she? It's too preposterous," Miss Glyde exclaimed.

"Listen." Miss Van Vluyck had repossessed herself of the *Encyclopedia*, and restored her spectacles to a nose reddened by excitement. " 'The Xingu, one of the principal rivers of Brazil, rises on the plateau of Mato Grosso, and flows in a northerly direction for a length of no less than one-thousand one-hundred eighteen miles, entering the Amazon near the mouth of the latter river. The upper course of the Xingu is auriferous and fed by numerous branches. Its source was first discovered in 1884 by the German explorer von den Steinen, after a difficult and dangerous expedition through a region inhabited by tribes still in the Stone Age of culture.' "

The ladies received this communication in a state of stupefied silence from which Mrs. Leveret was the first to rally. "She certainly *did* speak of its having branches."

The word seemed to snap the last thread of their incredulity. "And of its great length," gasped Mrs. Ballinger.

"She said it was awfully deep, and you couldn't skip — you just had to wade through," Miss Glyde added.

The idea worked its way more slowly through Mrs. Plinth's compact resistances. "How could there by anything improper about a river?" she inquired.

"Improper?"

"Why, what she said about the source — that it was corrupt?"

"Not corrupt, but hard to get at," Laura Glyde corrected. "Someone who'd been there had told her so. I dare say it was the explorer himself — doesn't it say the expedition was dangerous?"

" 'Difficult and dangerous,' " read Miss Van Vluyck.

Mrs. Ballinger pressed her hands to her throbbing temples. "There's nothing she said that wouldn't apply to a river — to this river!" She swung about excitedly to the other members. "Why, do you remember her telling us that she hadn't read *The Supreme Instant* because she'd taken it on a boating party while she was staying with her brother, and someone had 'shied' it overboard — 'shied' of course was her own expression."

The ladies breathlessly signified that the expression had not escaped them.

"Well — and then didn't she tell Osric Dane that one of her books was simply saturated with Xingu? Of course it was, if one of Mrs. Roby's rowdy friends had thrown it into the river!"

This surprising reconstruction of the scene in which they had just participated left the members of the Lunch Club inarticulate. At length, Mrs. Plinth, after visibly laboring with the problem, said in a heavy tone: "Osric Dane was taken in too."

Mrs. Leveret took courage at this. "Perhaps that's what Mrs. Roby did it for. She said Osric Dane was a brute, and she may have wanted to give her a lesson."

Miss Van Vluyck frowned. "It was hardly worthwhile to do it at our expense."

"At least," said Miss Glyde with a touch of bitterness, "she succeeded in interesting her, which was more than we did."

"What chance had we?" rejoined Mrs. Ballinger. "Mrs. Roby monopolized her from the first. And *that*, I've no doubt, was her purpose — to give Osric Dane a false impression of her own standing in the club. She would hesitate at nothing to attract attention: we all know how she took in poor Professor Foreland."

"She actually makes him give bridge teas every Thursday," Mrs. Leveret piped up.

Laura Glyde struck her hands together. "Why, this is Thursday, and it's *there* she's gone, of course; and taken Osric with her!"

"And they're shrieking over us at this moment," said Mrs. Ballinger between her teeth.

This possibility seemed too preposterous to be admitted. "She would hardly dare," said Miss Van Vluyck, "confess the imposture to Osric Dane."

"I'm not so sure: I thought I saw her make a sign as she left. If she hadn't made a sign, why should Osric Dane have rushed out after her?"

"Well, you know, we'd all been telling her how wonderful Xingu was, and she said she wanted to find out more about it," Mrs. Leveret said, with a tardy impulse of justice to the absent.

This reminder, far from mitigating the wrath of the other members, gave it a stronger impetus.

"Yes — and that's exactly what they're both laughing over now," said Laura Glyde ironically.

Mrs. Plinth stood up and gathered her expensive furs about her monumental form. "I have no wish to criticize," she said; "but unless the

Lunch Club can protect its members against the recurrence of such—such unbecoming scenes, I for one—"

"Oh, so do I!" agreed Miss Glyde, rising also.

Miss Van Vluyck closed the *Encyclopedia* and proceeded to button herself into her jacket. "My time is really too valuable—" she began.

"I fancy we are all of one mind," said Mrs. Ballinger, looking searchingly at Mrs. Leveret, who looked at the others.

"I always deprecate anything like a scandal—" Mrs. Plinth continued.

"She has been the cause of one today!" exclaimed Miss Glyde.

Mrs. Leveret moaned: "I don't see how she *could!*" and Miss Van Vluyck said, picking up her notebook: "Some women stop at nothing."

"—But if," Mrs. Plinth took up her argument impressively, "anything of the kind had happened in *my* house" (it never would have, her tone implied), "I should have felt that I owed it to myself either to ask for Mrs. Roby's resignation—or to offer mine."

"Oh, Mrs. Plinth—" gasped the Lunch Club.

"Fortunately for me," Mrs. Plinth continued with an awful magnanimity, "the matter was taken out of my hands by our President's decision that the right to entertain distinguished guests was a privilege vested in her office; and I think the other members will agree that, as she was alone in this opinion, she ought to be alone in deciding on the best way of effacing its—its really deplorable consequences."

A deep silence followed this outbreak of Mrs. Plinth's long-stored resentment.

"I don't see why *I* should be expected to ask her to resign—" Mrs. Ballinger at length began; but Laura Glyde turned back to remind her: "You know she made you say that you'd got on swimmingly in Xingu."

An ill-timed giggle escaped from Mrs. Leveret, and Mrs. Ballinger energetically continued "—But you needn't think for a moment that I'm afraid to!"

The door of the drawing room closed on the retreating backs of the Lunch Club, and the President of that distinguished association, seating herself at her writing table, and pushing away a copy of *The Wings of Death* to make room for her elbow, drew forth a sheet of the club's notepaper, on which she began to write: "My dear Mrs. Roby—"

The Other Two

I

WAYTHORN, on the drawing-room hearth, waited for his wife to come down to dinner.

It was their first night under his own roof, and he was surprised at his thrill of boyish agitation. He was not so old, to be sure — his glass gave him little more than the five-and-thirty years to which his wife confessed — but he had fancied himself already in the temperate zone; yet here he was listening for her step with a tender sense of all it symbolized, with some old trail of verse about the garlanded nuptial doorposts floating through his enjoyment of the pleasant room and the good dinner just beyond it.

They had been hastily recalled from their honeymoon by the illness of Lily Haskett, the child of Mrs. Waythorn's first marriage. The little girl, at Waythorn's desire, had been transferred to his house on the day of her mother's wedding, and the doctor, on their arrival, broke the news that she was ill with typhoid, but declared that all the symptoms were favorable. Lily could show twelve years of unblemished health, and the case promised to be a light one. The nurse spoke as reassuringly, and after a moment of alarm Mrs. Waythorn had adjusted herself to the situation. She was very fond of Lily — her affection for the child had perhaps been her decisive charm in Waythorn's eyes — but she had the perfectly balanced nerves which her little girl had inherited, and no woman ever wasted less tissue in unproductive worry. Waythorn was therefore quite prepared to see her come in presently, a little late because of a last look at Lily, but as serene and well-appointed as if her good-night kiss had been laid on the brow of health. Her composure was restful to him; it acted as ballast to his somewhat unstable sensibilities. As he pictured her bending over the child's bed he thought how soothing her presence must be in illness: her very step would prognosticate recovery.

His own life had been a gray one, from temperament rather than circumstance, and he had been drawn to her by the unperturbed gaiety which kept her fresh and elastic at an age when most women's activities are growing either slack or febrile. He knew what was said about her; for, popular as she was, there had always been a faint undercurrent of detraction. When she had appeared in New York, nine or ten years earlier, as the pretty Mrs. Haskett whom Gus Varick had unearthed somewhere — was it in Pittsburgh or Utica? — society, while promptly accepting her, had reserved the right to cast a doubt on its own indiscrimination. Inquiry, however, established her undoubted connection with a socially reigning family, and explained her recent divorce as the natural result of a runaway match at seventeen; and as nothing was known of Mr. Haskett it was easy to believe the worst of him.

Alice Haskett's remarriage with Gus Varick was a passport to the set whose recognition she coveted, and for a few years the Varicks were the most popular couple in town. Unfortunately the alliance was brief and stormy, and this time the husband had his champions. Still, even Varick's stanchest supporters admitted that he was not meant for matrimony, and Mrs. Varick's grievances were of a nature to bear the inspection of the New York courts. A New York divorce is in itself a diploma of virtue, and in the semiwidowhood of this second separation Mrs. Varick took on an air of sanctity, and was allowed to confide her wrongs to some of the most scrupulous ears in town. But when it was known that she was to marry Waythorn there was a momentary reaction. Her best friends would have preferred to see her remain in the role of the injured wife, which was as becoming to her as crepe to a rosy complexion. True, a decent time had elapsed, and it was not even suggested that Waythorn had supplanted his predecessor. People shook their heads over him, however, and one grudging friend, to whom he affirmed that he took the step with his eyes open, replied oracularly: "Yes — and with your ears shut."

Waythorn could afford to smile at these innuendoes. In the Wall Street phrase, he had "discounted" them. He knew that society has not yet adapted itself to the consequences of divorce, and that till the adaptation takes place every woman who uses the freedom the law accords her must be her own social justification. Waythorn had an amused confidence in his wife's ability to justify herself. His expectations were fulfilled, and before the wedding took place Alice Varick's group had rallied openly to her support. She took it all imperturbably: she had a way of surmounting obstacles without seeming to be aware of them, and Waythorn looked back with wonder at the trivialities over which he had worn his nerves thin. He had the sense of having found refuge in a richer, warmer nature than his own, and his satisfaction, at the moment, was humorously summed up in the thought that his wife, when she had done all she could for Lily, would not be ashamed to come down and enjoy a good dinner.

The anticipation of such enjoyment was not, however, the sentiment expressed by Mrs. Waythorn's charming face when she presently joined him. Though she had put on her most engaging tea gown she had neglected to assume the smile that went with it, and Waythorn thought he had never seen her look so nearly worried.

"What is it?" he asked. "Is anything wrong with Lily?"

"No; I've just been in and she's still sleeping." Mrs. Waythorn hesitated. "But something tiresome has happened."

He had taken her two hands, and now perceived that he was crushing a paper between them.

"This letter?"

"Yes — Mr. Haskett has written — I mean his lawyer has written."

Waythorn felt himself flush uncomfortably. He dropped his wife's hands.

"What about?"

"About seeing Lily. You know the courts —"

"Yes, yes," he interrupted nervously.

Nothing was known about Haskett in New York. He was vaguely supposed to have remained in the outer darkness from which his wife had been rescued, and Waythorn was one of the few who were aware that he had given up his business in Utica and followed her to New York in order to be near his little girl. In the days of his wooing, Waythorn had often met Lily on the doorstep, rosy and smiling, on her way "to see papa."

"I am so sorry," Mrs. Waythorn murmured.

He roused himself. "What does he want?"

"He wants to see her. You know she goes to him once a week."

"Well — he doesn't expect her to go to him now, does he?"

"No — he has heard of her illness; but he expects to come here."

"*Here?*"

Mrs. Waythorn reddened under his gaze. They looked away from each other.

"I'm afraid he has the right . . . You'll see. . . ." She made a proffer of the letter.

Waythorn moved away with a gesture of refusal. He stood staring about the softly-lighted room, which a moment before had seemed so full of bridal intimacy.

"I'm so sorry," she repeated. "If Lily could have been moved —"

"That's out of the question," he returned impatiently.

"I suppose so."

Her lip was beginning to tremble, and he felt himself a brute.

"He must come, of course," he said. "When is — his day?"

"I'm afraid — tomorrow."

"Very well. Send a note in the morning."

The butler entered to announce dinner.

Waythorn turned to his wife. "Come — you must be tired. It's beastly, but try to forget about it," he said, drawing her hand through his arm.

"You're so good, dear. I'll try," she whispered back.

Her face cleared at once, and as she looked at him across the flowers, between the rosy candleshades, he saw her lips waver back into a smile.

"How pretty everything is!" she sighed luxuriously.

He turned to the butler. "The champagne at once, please. Mrs. Waythorn is tired."

In a moment or two their eyes met above the sparkling glasses. Her own were quite clear and untroubled: he saw that she had obeyed his injunction and forgotten.

II

Waythorn, the next morning, went downtown earlier than usual. Haskett was not likely to come till the afternoon, but the instinct of flight drove him forth. He meant to stay away all day — he had thoughts of dining at his club. As his door closed behind him he reflected that before he opened it again it would have admitted another man who had as much right to enter it as himself, and the thought filled him with a physical repugnance.

He caught the elevated at the employees' hour, and found himself crushed between two layers of pendulous humanity. At Eighth Street the man facing him wriggled out, and another took his place. Waythorn glanced up and saw that it was Gus Varick. The men were so close together that it was impossible to ignore the smile of recognition on Varick's handsome overblown face. And after all — why not? They had always been on good terms, and Varick had been divorced before Waythorn's attentions to his wife began. The two exchanged a word on the perennial grievance of the congested trains, and when a seat at their side was miraculously left empty the instinct of self-preservation made Waythorn slip into it after Varick.

The latter drew the stout man's breath of relief. "Lord—I was beginning to feel like a pressed flower." He leaned back, looking unconcernedly at Waythorn. "Sorry to hear that Sellers is knocked out again."

"Sellers?" echoed Waythorn, starting at his partner's name.

Varick looked surprised. "You didn't know he was laid up with the gout?"

"No. I've been away—I only got back last night." Waythorn felt himself reddening in anticipation of the other's smile.

"Ah—yes; to be sure. And Sellers' attack came on two days ago. I'm afraid he's pretty bad. Very awkward for me, as it happens, because he was just putting through a rather important thing for me."

"Ah?" Waythorn wondered vaguely since when Varick had been dealing in "important things." Hitherto he had dabbled only in the shallow pools of speculation, with which Waythorn's office did not usually concern itself.

It occurred to him that Varick might be talking at random, to relieve the strain of their propinquity. That strain was becoming momentarily more apparent to Waythorn, and when, at Cortlandt Street, he caught sight of an acquaintance and had a sudden vision of the picture he and Varick must present to an initiated eye, he jumped up with a muttered excuse.

"I hope you'll find Sellers better," said Varick civilly, and he stammered back: "If I can be of any use to you—" and let the departing crowd sweep him to the platform.

At his office he heard that Sellers was in fact ill with the gout, and would probably not be able to leave the house for some weeks.

"I'm sorry it should have happened so, Mr. Waythorn," the senior clerk said with affable significance. "Mr. Sellers was very much upset at the idea of giving you such a lot of extra work just now."

"Oh, that's no matter," said Waythorn hastily. He secretly welcomed the pressure of additional business, and was glad to think that, when the day's work was over, he would have to call at his partner's on the way home.

He was late for luncheon, and turned in at the nearest restaurant instead of going to his club. The place was full, and the waiter hurried him to the back of the room to capture the only vacant table. In the cloud of cigar smoke Waythorn did not at once distinguish his neighbors: but presently, looking about him, he saw Varick seated a few feet off. This time, luckily, they were too far apart for conversation, and

Varick, who faced another way, had probably not even seen him; but there was an irony in their renewed nearness.

Varick was said to be fond of good living, and as Waythorn sat dispatching his hurried luncheon he looked across half enviously at the other's leisurely degustation of his meal. When Waythorn first saw him he had been helping himself with critical deliberation to a bit of Camembert at the ideal point of liquefaction, and now, the cheese removed, he was just pouring his *café double*[1] from its little two-storied earthen pot. He poured slowly, his ruddy profile bent over the task, and one beringed white hand steadying the lid of the coffeepot; then he streched his other hand to the decanter of cognac at his elbow, filled a liqueur glass, took a tentative sip, and poured the brandy into his coffee cup.

Waythorn watched him in a kind of fascination. What was he thinking of — only of the flavor of the coffee and the liqueur? Had the morning's meeting left no more trace in his thoughts than on his face? Had his wife so completely passed out of his life that even this odd encounter with her present husband, within a week after her remarriage, was no more than an incident in his day? And as Waythorn mused, another idea struck him: had Haskett ever met Varick as Varick and he had just met? The recollection of Haskett perturbed him, and he rose and left the restaurant, taking a circuitous way out to escape the placid irony of Varick's nod.

It was after seven when Waythorn reached home. He thought the footman who opened the door looked at him oddly.

"How is Miss Lily?" he asked in haste.

"Doing very well, sir. A gentleman —"

"Tell Barlow to put off dinner for half an hour," Waythorn cut him off, hurrying upstairs.

He went straight to his room and dressed without seeing his wife. When he reached the drawing room she was there, fresh and radiant. Lily's day had been good; the doctor was not coming back that evening.

At dinner Waythorn told her of Sellers' illness and of the resulting complications. She listened sympathetically, adjuring him not to let himself be overworked, and asking vague feminine questions about the routine of the office. Then she gave him the chronicle of Lily's day; quoted the nurse and doctor, and told him who had called to inquire. He had never seen her more serene and unruffled. It struck him with a curious pang, that she was very happy in being with him, so happy that she found a childish pleasure in rehearsing the trivial incidents of her day.

1. *café double*] very strong coffee.

After dinner they went to the library, and the servant put the coffee and liqueurs on a low table before her and left the room. She looked singularly soft and girlish in her rosy-pale dress, against the dark leather of one of his bachelor armchairs. A day earlier the contrast would have charmed him.

He turned away now, choosing a cigar with affected deliberation.

"Did Haskett come?" he asked, with his back to her.

"Oh, yes—he came."

"You didn't see him, of course?"

She hesitated a moment. "I let the nurse see him."

That was all. There was nothing more to ask. He swung round toward her, applying a match to his cigar. Well, the thing was over for a week, at any rate. He would try not to think of it. She looked up at him, a trifle rosier than usual, with a smile in her eyes.

"Ready for your coffee, dear?"

He leaned against the mantelpiece, watching her as she lifted the coffeepot. The lamplight struck a gleam from her bracelets and tipped her soft hair with brightness. How light and slender she was, and how each gesture flowed into the next! She seemed a creature all compact of harmonies. As the thought of Haskett receded, Waythorn felt himself yielding again to the joy of possessorship. They were his, those white hands with their flitting motions, his the light haze of hair, the lips and eyes. . . .

She set down the coffeepot, and reaching for the decanter of cognac, measured off a liqueur glass and poured it into his cup.

Waythorn uttered a sudden exclamation.

"What is the matter?" she said, startled.

"Nothing; only—I don't take cognac in my coffee."

"Oh, how stupid of me," she cried.

Their eyes met, and she blushed a sudden agonized red.

III

Ten days later, Mr. Sellers, still housebound, asked Waythorn to call on his way downtown.

The senior partner, with his swaddled foot propped up by the fire, greeted his associate with an air of embarrassment.

"I'm sorry, my dear fellow; I've got to ask you to do an awkward thing for me."

Waythorn waited, and the other went on, after a pause apparently given to the arrangement of his phrases: "The fact is, when I was knocked out I had just gone into a rather complicated piece of business for — Gus Varick."

"Well?" said Waythorn, with an attempt to put him at his ease.

"Well — it's this way: Varick came to me the day before my attack. He had evidently had an inside tip from somebody, and had made about a hundred thousand. He came to me for advice, and I suggested his going in with Vanderlyn."

"Oh, the deuce!" Waythorn exclaimed. He saw in a flash what had happened. The investment was an alluring one, but required negotiation. He listened quietly while Sellers put the case before him, and, the statement ended, he said: "You think I ought to see Varick?"

"I'm afraid I can't as yet. The doctor is obdurate. And this thing can't wait. I hate to ask you, but no one else in the office knows the ins and outs of it."

Waythorn stood silent. He did not care a farthing for the success of Varick's venture, but the honor of the office was to be considered, and he could hardly refuse to oblige his partner.

"Very well," he said, "I'll do it."

That afternoon, apprised by telephone, Varick called at the office. Waythorn, waiting in his private room, wondered what the others thought of it. The newspapers, at the time of Mrs. Waythorn's marriage, had acquainted their readers with every detail of her previous matrimonial ventures, and Waythorn could fancy the clerks smiling behind Varick's back as he was ushered in.

Varick bore himself admirably. He was easy without being undignified, and Waythorn was conscious of cutting a much less impressive figure. Varick had no experience of business, and the talk prolonged itself for nearly an hour while Waythorn set forth with scrupulous precision the details of the proposed transaction.

"I'm awfully obliged to you," Varick said as he rose. "The fact is I'm not used to having much money to look after, and I don't want to make an ass of myself—" He smiled, and Waythorn could not help noticing that there was something pleasant about his smile. "It feels uncommonly queer to have enough cash to pay one's bills. I'd have sold my soul for it a few years ago!"

Waythorn winced at the allusion. He had heard it rumored that a lack of funds had been one of the determining causes of the Varick separation, but it did not occur to him that Varick's words were intentional. It seemed more likely that the desire to keep clear of embarrassing topics had fatally drawn him into one. Waythorn did not wish to be outdone in civility.

"We'll do the best we can for you," he said. "I think this is a good thing you're in."

"Oh, I'm sure it's immense. It's awfully good of you—" Varick broke off, embarrassed. "I suppose the thing's settled now—but if—"

"If anything happens before Sellers is about, I'll see you again," said Waythorn quietly. He was glad, in the end, to appear the more self-possessed of the two.

The course of Lily's illness ran smooth, and as the days passed Waythorn grew used to the idea of Haskett's weekly visit. The first time the day came round, he stayed out late, and questioned his wife as to the visit on his return. She replied at once that Haskett had merely seen the nurse downstairs, as the doctor did not wish anyone in the child's sickroom till after the crisis.

The following week Waythorn was again conscious of the recurrence of the day, but had forgotten it by the time he came home to dinner. The crisis of the disease came a few days later, with a rapid decline of fever, and the little girl was pronounced out of danger. In the rejoicing which ensued the thought of Haskett passed out of Waythorn's mind, and one afternoon, letting himself into the house with a latchkey, he went straight to his library without noticing a shabby hat and umbrella in the hall.

In the library he found a small effaced-looking man with a thinnish gray beard sitting on the edge of a chair. The stranger might have been a piano tuner, or one of those mysteriously efficient persons who are summoned in emergencies to adjust some detail of the domestic machinery. He blinked at Waythorn through a pair of gold-rimmed spectacles and said mildly: "Mr. Waythorn, I presume? I am Lily's father."

Waythorn flushed. "Oh—" he stammered uncomfortably. He broke off, disliking to appear rude. Inwardly he was trying to adjust the actual Haskett to the image of him projected by his wife's reminiscences. Waythorn had been allowed to infer that Alice's first husband was a brute.

"I am sorry to intrude," said Haskett, with his over-the-counter politeness.

"Don't mention it," returned Waythorn, collecting himself. "I suppose the nurse has been told?"

"I presume so. I can wait," said Haskett. He had a resigned way of speaking, as though life had worn down his natural powers of resistance.

Waythorn stood on the threshold, nervously pulling off his gloves. "I'm sorry you've been detained. I will send for the nurse," he said; and as he opened the door he added with an effort: "I'm glad we can give you a good report of Lily." He winced as the *we* slipped out, but Haskett seemed not to notice it.

"Thank you, Mr. Waythorn, it's been an anxious time for me."

"Ah, well, that's past. Soon she'll be able to go to you." Waythorn nodded and passed out.

In his own room he flung himself down with a groan. He hated the womanish sensibility which made him suffer so acutely from the grotesque chances of life. He had known when he married that his wife's former husbands were both living, and that amid the multiplied contacts of modern existence there were a thousand chances to one that he would run against one or the other, yet he found himself as much disturbed by his brief encounter with Haskett as though the law had not obligingly removed all difficulties in the way of their meeting.

Waythorn sprang up and began to pace the room nervously. He had not suffered half as much from his two meetings with Varick. It was Haskett's presence in his own house that made the situation so intolerable. He stood still, hearing steps in the passage.

"This way, please," he heard the nurse say. Haskett was being taken upstairs, then: not a corner of the house but was open to him. Waythorn dropped into another chair, staring vaguely ahead of him. On his dressing table stood a photograph of Alice, taken when he had first known her. She was Alice Varick then — how fine and exquisite he had thought her! Those were Varick's pearls about her neck. At Waythorn's instance they had been returned before her marriage. Had Haskett ever given her any trinkets — and what had become of them, Waythorn wondered? He realized suddenly that he knew very little of Haskett's past or present situation; but from the man's appearance and manner of speech he could reconstruct with curious precision the surroundings of Alice's first marriage. And it startled him to think that she had, in the background of her life, a phase of existence so different from anything with which he had connected her. Varick, whatever his faults, was a gentleman, in the conventional, traditional sense of the term: the sense which at that moment seemed, oddly enough, to have most meaning to Waythorn. He and Varick had the same social habits, spoke the same language, understood the same allusions. But this other man . . . it was grotesquely uppermost in Waythorn's mind that Haskett had worn a made-up tie attached with an elastic. Why should that ridiculous detail symbolize the whole man? Waythorn was exasperated by his own paltriness, but the fact of the tie expanded, forced itself on him, became as it were the key to Alice's past. He could see her, as Mrs. Haskett, sitting in a "front parlor" furnished in plush, with a pianola, and copy of *Ben Hur* on the center table. He could see her going to the theater with Haskett — or perhaps even to a "Church Sociable" — she in a "picture hat" and Haskett in a black frock coat, a little creased, with the made-up tie on an elastic. On the way home they would stop and look at the illuminated shop windows, lingering over the photographs of New York actresses. On Sunday afternoons Haskett would take her for a walk, pushing Lily ahead of them in a white enameled perambulator, and Waythorn had a vision of the people they would stop and talk to. He could fancy how pretty Alice must have looked, in a dress adroitly constructed from the hints of a New York fashion paper, and how she must have looked down on the other women, chafing at her life, and secretly feeling that she belonged in a bigger place.

For the moment his foremost thought was one of wonder at the way in which she had shed the phase of existence which her marriage with Haskett implied. It was as if her whole aspect, every gesture, every inflection, every allusion, were a studied negation of that period of her life. If she had denied being married to Haskett she could hardly have stood more convicted of duplicity than in this obliteration of the self which had been his wife.

Waythorn started up, checking himself in the analysis of her motives. What right had he to create a fantastic effigy of her and then pass judgment on it? She had spoken vaguely of her first marriage as unhappy, had hinted, with becoming reticence, that Haskett had wrought havoc among her young illusions. . . . It was a pity for Waythorn's peace of mind that Haskett's very inoffensiveness shed a new light on the nature of those illusions. A man would rather think that his wife has been brutalized by her first husband than that the process has been reversed.

IV

"Mr. Waythorn, I don't like that French governess of Lily's."

Haskett, subdued and apologetic, stood before Waythorn in the library, revolving his shabby hat in his hand.

Waythorn, surprised in his armchair over the evening paper, stared back perplexedly at his visitor.

"You'll excuse my asking to see you," Haskett continued. "But this is my last visit, and I thought if I could have a word with you it would be a better way than writing to Mrs. Waythorn's lawyer."

Waythorn rose uneasily. He did not like the French governess either; but that was irrelevant.

"I am not so sure of that," he returned stiffly; "but since you wish it I will give your message to — my wife." He always hesitated over the possessive pronoun in addressing Haskett.

The latter sighed. "I don't know as that will help much. She didn't like it when I spoke to her."

Waythorn turned red. "When did you see her?" he asked.

"Not since the first day I came to see Lily — right after she was taken sick. I remarked to her then that I didn't like the governess."

Waythorn made no answer. He remembered distinctly that, after that first visit, he had asked his wife if she had seen Haskett. She had lied to him then, but she had respected his wishes since; and the incident cast a curious light on her character. He was sure she would not have seen Haskett that first day if she had divined that Waythorn would object, and the fact that she did not divine it was almost as disagreeable to the latter as the discovery that she had lied to him.

"I don't like the woman," Haskett was repeating with mild persistency. "She ain't straight, Mr. Waythorn — she'll teach the child to be underhand. I've noticed a change in Lily — she's too anxious to please — and she don't always tell the truth. She used to be the straightest child. Mr. Waythorn —" He broke off, his voice a little thick. "Not but what I want her to have a stylish education," he ended.

Waythorn was touched. "I'm sorry, Mr. Haskett; but frankly, I don't quite see what I can do."

Haskett hesitated. Then he laid his hat on the table, and advanced to the hearthrug, on which Waythorn was standing. There was nothing aggressive in his manner, but he had the solemnity of a timid man resolved on a decisive measure.

"There's just one thing you can do, Mr. Waythorn," he said. "You can remind Mrs. Waythorn that, by the decree of the courts, I am entitled to have a voice in Lily's bringing-up." He paused, and went on more deprecatingly: "I am not the kind to talk about enforcing my rights, Mr. Waythorn. I don't know as I think a man is entitled to rights he hasn't known how to hold on to; but this business of the child is different. I've never let go there — and I never mean to."

The scene left Waythorn deeply shaken. Shamefacedly, in indirect ways, he had been finding out about Haskett; and all that he had learned was favorable. The little man, in order to be near his daughter, had sold out his share in a profitable business in Utica, and accepted a modest clerkship in a New York manufacturing house. He boarded in a shabby street and had few acquaintances. His passion for Lily filled his life. Waythorn felt that this exploration of Haskett was like groping about with a dark lantern in his wife's past; but he saw now that there were recesses his lantern had not explored. He had never inquired into the exact circumstances of his wife's first matrimonial rupture. On the surface all had been fair. It was she who had obtained the divorce, and the court had given her the child. But Waythorn knew how many ambiguities such a verdict might cover. The mere fact that Haskett retained a right over his daughter implied an unsuspected compromise. Waythorn was an idealist. He always refused to recognize unpleasant contingencies till he found himself confronted with them, and then he saw them followed by a spectral train of consequences. His next days were thus haunted, and he determined to try to lay the ghosts by conjuring them up in his wife's presence.

When he repeated Haskett's request a flame of anger passed over her face; but she subdued it instantly and spoke with a slight quiver of outraged motherhood.

"It is very ungentlemanly of him," she said.

The word grated on Waythorn. "That is neither here nor there. It's a bare question of rights."

She murmured: "It's not as if he could ever be a help to Lily—"

Waythorn flushed. This was even less to his taste. "The question is," he repeated, "what authority has he over her?"

She looked downward, twisting herself a little in her seat. "I am willing to see him—I thought you objected," she faltered.

In a flash he understood that she knew the extent of Haskett's claims. Perhaps it was not the first time she had resisted them.

"My objecting has nothing to do with it," he said coldly; "if Haskett has a right to be consulted you must consult him."

She burst into tears, and he saw that she expected him to regard her as a victim.

Haskett did not abuse his rights. Waythorn had felt miserably sure that he would not. But the governess was dismissed, and from time to time the little man demanded an interview with Alice. After the first outburst she accepted the situation with her usual adaptability. Haskett had once reminded Waythorn of the piano tuner, and Mrs. Waythorn, after a month or two, appeared to class him with that domestic familiar. Waythorn could not but respect the father's tenacity. At first he had tried to cultivate the suspicion that Haskett might be "up to" something, that he had an object in securing a foothold in the house. But in his heart

Waythorn was sure of Haskett's single-mindedness; he even guessed in the latter a mild contempt for such advantages as his relation with the Waythorns might offer. Haskett's sincerity of purpose made him invulnerable, and his successor had to accept him as a lien on the property.

Mr. Sellers was sent to Europe to recover from his gout, and Varick's affairs hung on Waythorn's hands. The negotiations were prolonged and complicated; they necessitated frequent conferences between the two men, and the interests of the firm forbade Waythorn's suggesting that his client should transfer his business to another office.

Varick appeared well in the transaction. In moments of relaxation his coarse streak appeared, and Waythorn dreaded his geniality; but in the office he was concise and clear-headed, with a flattering deference to Waythorn's judgment. Their business relations being so affably established, it would have been absurd for the two men to ignore each other in society. The first time they met in a drawing room, Varick took up their intercourse in the same easy key, and his hostess' grateful glance obliged Waythorn to respond to it. After that they ran across each other frequently, and one evening at a ball Waythorn, wandering through the remoter rooms, came upon Varick seated beside his wife. She colored a little, and faltered in what she was saying; but Varick nodded to Waythorn without rising, and the latter strolled on.

In the carriage, on the way home, he broke out nervously: "I didn't know you spoke to Varick."

Her voice trembled a little. "It's the first time — he happened to be standing near me; I didn't know what to do. It's so awkward, meeting everywhere — and he said you had been very kind about some business."

"That's different," said Waythorn.

She paused a moment. "I'll do just as you wish," she returned pliantly. "I thought it would be less awkward to speak to him when we meet."

Her pliancy was beginning to sicken him. Had she really no will of her own — no theory about her relation to these men? She had accepted Haskett — did she mean to accept Varick? It was "less awkward," as she had said, and her instinct was to evade difficulties or to circumvent them. With sudden vividness Waythorn saw how the instinct had developed. She was "as easy as an old shoe" — a shoe that too many feet had worn. Her elasticity was the result of tension in too many different directions. Alice Haskett — Alice Varick — Alice Waythorn — she had been each in turn, and had left hanging to each name a little of her privacy, a little of her personality, a little of the inmost self where the unknown god abides.

"Yes—it's better to speak to Varick," said Waythorn wearily.

V

The winter wore on, and society took advantage of the Waythorns' acceptance of Varick. Harassed hostesses were grateful to them for bridging over a social difficulty, and Mrs. Waythorn was held up as a miracle of good taste. Some experimental spirits could not resist the diversion of throwing Varick and his former wife together, and there were those who thought he found a zest in the propinquity. But Mrs. Waythorn's conduct remained irreproachable. She neither avoided Varick nor sought him out. Even Waythorn could not but admit that she had discovered the solution of the newest social problem.

He had married her without giving much thought to that problem. He had fancied that a woman can shed her past like a man. But now he saw that Alice was bound to hers both by the circumstances which forced her into continued relation with it, and by the traces it had left on her nature. With grim irony Waythorn compared himself to a member of a syndicate. He held so many shares in his wife's personality and his predecessors were his partners in the business. If there had been any element of passion in the transaction he would have felt less deteriorated by it. The fact that Alice took her change of husbands like a change of weather reduced the situation to mediocrity. He could have forgiven her for blunders, for excesses: for resisting Haskett, for yielding to Varick; for anything but her acquiescence and her tact. She reminded him of a juggler tossing knives; but the knives were blunt and she knew they would never cut her.

And then, gradually, habit formed a protecting surface for his sensibilities. If he paid for each day's comfort with the small change of his illusions, he grew daily to value the comfort more and set less store upon the coin. He had drifted into a dulling propinquity with Haskett and Varick and he took refuge in the cheap revenge of satirizing the situation. He even began to reckon up the advantages which accrued from it, to ask himself if it were not better to own a third of a wife who knew how to make a man happy than a whole one who had lacked opportunity to acquire the art. For it *was* an art, and made up, like all others, of concessions, eliminations and embellishments; of lights judiciously thrown and shadows skillfully softened. His wife knew exactly how to manage the lights, and he knew exactly to what training she owed her skill. He even tried to trace the source of his obligations, to discriminate between the influences which had combined to produce his domestic happiness: he perceived that Haskett's commonness had made Alice worship good breeding, while Varick's liberal construction of the marriage bond had taught her to value the conjugal virtues; so that he was directly indebted to his predecessors for the devotion which made his life easy if not inspiring.

From this phase he passed into that of complete acceptance. He ceased to satirize himself because time dulled the irony of the situation and the joke lost its humor with its sting. Even the sight of Haskett's hat on the hall table had ceased to touch the springs of epigram. The hat was often seen there now, for it had been decided that it was better for Lily's father to visit her than for the little girl to go to his boardinghouse. Waythorn, having acquiesced in this arrangement, had been surprised to find how little difference it made. Haskett was never obtrusive, and the few visitors who met him on the stairs were unaware of his identity. Waythorn did not know how often he saw Alice, but with himself Haskett was seldom in contact.

One afternoon, however, he learned on entering that Lily's father was waiting to see him. In the library he found Haskett occupying a chair in his usual provisional way. Waythorn always felt grateful to him for not leaning back.

"I hope you'll excuse me, Mr. Waythorn," he said rising. "I wanted to see Mrs. Waythorn about Lily, and your man asked me to wait here till she came in."

"Of course," said Waythorn, remembering that a sudden leak had that morning given over the drawing room to the plumbers.

He opened his cigar case and held it out to his visitor, and Haskett's acceptance seemed to mark a fresh stage in their intercourse. The spring evening was chilly, and Waythorn invited his guest to draw up his chair to the fire. He meant to find an excuse to leave Haskett in a moment; but he was tired and cold, and after all the little man no longer jarred on him.

The two were enclosed in the intimacy of their blended cigar smoke when the door opened and Varick walked into the room. Waythorn rose abruptly. It was the first time that Varick had come to the house, and the surprise of seeing him, combined with the singular inopportuneness of his arrival, gave a new edge to Waythorn's blunted sensibilities. He stared at his visitor without speaking.

Varick seemed too preoccupied to notice his host's embarrassment. "My dear fellow," he exclaimed in his most expansive tone, "I must apologize for tumbling in on you in this way, but I was too late to catch you downtown, and so I thought—"

He stopped short, catching sight of Haskett, and his sanguine color deepened to a flush which spread vividly under his scant blond hair. But in a moment he recovered himself and nodded slightly. Haskett returned the bow in silence, and Waythorn was still groping for speech when the footman came in carrying a tea table.

The intrusion offered a welcome vent to Waythorn's nerves. "What the deuce are you bringing this here for?" he said sharply.

"I beg your pardon, sir, but the plumbers are still in the drawing room, and Mrs. Waythorn said she would have tea in the library." The footman's perfectly respectful tone implied a reflection on Waythorn's reasonableness.

"Oh, very well," said the latter resignedly, and the footman proceeded to open the folding tea table and set out its complicated appointments. While this interminable process continued the three men stood motionless, watching it with a fascinated stare, till Waythorn, to break the silence, said to Varick, "Won't you have a cigar?"

He held out the case he had just tendered to Haskett, and Varick helped himself with a smile. Waythorn looked about for a match, and finding none, proffered a light from his own cigar. Haskett, in the background, held his ground mildly, examining his cigar tip now and then, and stepping forward at the right moment to knock its ashes into the fire.

The footman at last withdrew, and Varick immediately began: "If I could just say half a word to you about this business—"

"Certainly," stammered Waythorn; "in the dining room—"

But as he placed his hand on the door it opened from without, and his wife appeared on the threshold.

She came in fresh and smiling, in her street dress and hat, shedding a fragrance from the boa which she loosened in advancing.

"Shall we have tea in here, dear?" she began; and then she caught sight of Varick. Her smile deepened, veiling a slight tremor of surprise.

"Why, how do you do?" she said with a distinct note of pleasure.

As she shook hands with Varick she saw Haskett standing behind him. Her smile faded for a moment, but she recalled it quickly, with a scarcely perceptible side glance at Waythorn.

"How do you do, Mr. Haskett?" she said, and shook hands with him a shade less cordially.

The three men stood awkwardly before her, till Varick, always the most self-possessed, dashed into an explanatory phrase.

"We — I had to see Waythorn a moment on business," he stammered, brick-red from chin to nape.

Haskett stepped forward with his air of mild obstinacy. "I am sorry to intrude; but you appointed five o'clock —" he directed his resigned glance to the timepiece on the mantel.

She swept aside their embarrassment with a charming gesture of hospitality.

"I'm so sorry — I'm always late; but the afternoon was so lovely." She stood drawing off her gloves, propitiatory and graceful, diffusing about her a sense of ease and familiarity in which the situation lost its grotesqueness. "But before talking business," she added brightly, "I'm sure everyone wants a cup of tea."

She dropped into her low chair by the tea table, and the two visitors, as if drawn by her smile, advanced to receive the cups she held out.

She glanced about for Waythorn, and he took the third cup with a laugh.